HEARTS *of* STONE

HEARTS *of* STONE

Kathleen Ernst

DUTTON CHILDREN'S BOOKS

DUTTON CHILDREN'S BOOKS
A division of Penguin Young Readers Group
Published by the Penguin Group
Penguin Group (USA) Inc., 375 Hudson Street, New York, New York 10014, U.S.A.
Penguin Group (Canada), 90 Eglinton Avenue East, Suite 700, Toronto, Ontario,
Canada M4P 2Y3 (a division of Pearson Penguin Canada Inc.)
Penguin Books Ltd, 80 Strand, London WC2R 0RL, England
Penguin Ireland, 25 St Stephen's Green, Dublin 2, Ireland (a division of Penguin Books
Ltd)
Penguin Group (Australia), 250 Camberwell Road, Camberwell, Victoria 3124,
Australia (a division of Pearson Australia Group Pty Ltd)
Penguin Books India Pvt Ltd, 11 Community Centre, Panchsheel Park, New Delhi -
110 017, India
Penguin Group (NZ), Cnr Airborne and Rosedale Roads, Albany, Auckland 1310,
New Zealand (a division of Pearson New Zealand Ltd)
Penguin Books (South Africa) (Pty) Ltd, 24 Sturdee Avenue, Rosebank, Johannesburg
2196, South Africa
Penguin Books Ltd, Registered Offices: 80 Strand, London WC2R 0RL, England

CIP Data is available.

Published in the United States by Dutton Children's Books,
a division of Penguin Young Readers Group
345 Hudson Street, New York, New York 10014
www.penguin.com/youngreaders

Designed by Irene Vandervoort
Printed in USA   First Edition
ISBN 0-525-47686-5
10 9 8 7 6 5 4 3 2 1

This book about *family*
is for my own.

Acknowledgments

In 1995, a huge Civil War reenactment took place in Spring Hill, Tennessee. It was my great good fortune to participate in a small refugee camp scenario organized by the Ladies' Soldiers' Friends Society. While thousands of military reenactors took to the field, we did our best to re-create an authentic civilian refugee camp based on accounts left behind in Nashville newspapers, letters, reminiscences, and military records. Most of us slept in small tents (although a hardy few endured Friday's cold, torrential rain under makeshift shelters), and our period-appropriate food was prepared over open fires. The seed for this novel was planted that weekend, and I am indebted to Refugee Coordinator Libby Smith, researcher Vicki Betts, and the other organizers and participants who provided such a rich experience.

This novel had an unusually long gestation, but the Writer Chicks on the Road, past and present, pretended not to mind reading dozens of drafts over the years. Eileen Daily, Marsha Dunlap, Amy Laundrie, Katie Mead, Julia Pferdehirt, and Gayle Rosengren—I'm thankful for your friendship, suggestions, and support.

Thanks to my agent, Andrea Cascardi, for believing in this story. I'll forever be grateful to Michele Coppola for bringing *Hearts of Stone* to Dutton, Stephanie Owens Lurie for keeping it there, and Maureen Sullivan, my wonderful editor, who asked all the right questions.

I've been blessed with a supportive family all around. And special thanks to my husband, Scott, for his unwavering faith.

HEARTS *of* STONE

⚓ **1861** ⚓

Pa ripped our family apart just as spring began whispering sweet promises up on Cumberland Mountain. Serviceberry buds swelled fuzzy and silver. A red fox birthed five kits in an old woodchuck burrow near the meadow. Fiddlehead ferns uncurled by the springhouse. At dawn and twilight, wrens sang their pretty *come-to-me, come-to-me* song from the fence rails.

And the frost wriggled out of our corn patch, bringing a new crop of stones to light as it went. On one of those warm-in-the-sun, cool-in-the-shade afternoons I put the twins down to nap on a blanket while my little brother, Jasper, and I picked stones. I stopped when I heard Maude laughing. She was dancing after a yellow butterfly, soft fingers outstretched, her joy bubbling out like a stream blessed with new rain.

"Keep an eye on Mary," I told Jasper. "She'll likely wake soon. I'll go fetch some corn bread, and we'll take a break."

My back complained as I stepped onto the porch, so I stopped to stretch out a kink. But my feet chose to plant themselves right there when I heard Mama and Pa arguing inside the cabin.

"I'm fixing to go," Pa was saying. "And there's a few other men of like mind. We're thinking to leave next week."

Mama's voice edged like an ax. "Your family needs you."

"I know that," he said. "But the army needs me more."

All that frost got sucked right into my gut.

Folks in East Tennessee had been making a fuss about Mr. Lincoln's war for weeks. Some believed in the Union that the Yankee soldiers were trying to hold together. Some cheered when Tennessee joined the new Confederacy of Southern states. Some had no tolerance for either side. I'd never heard Pa speak about it in particular. I didn't even know which army he thought to join.

Mama's rocking chair began to creak, faster and faster. "You'd leave this place. You'd leave your wife and children."

"The Yankees will come take charge of East Tennessee," Pa said. "And I'll come home with 'em. Sometimes a man just knows when a thing's got to be done. This is one of those times. We Camerons know the difference between right and wrong."

I heard a sound behind me—Jasper, come after his corn bread. His eyes had gone wide.

Mama's voice was low and cold. "So you men are going to run off and have yourselves a fine adventure." *Creak, creak.* "Well, never you mind about your family, then. *I'll* guard this hearth. *I'll* hold this family together." *Creak-creak-creak!* "Don't speak to me of a thing that's got to be done, Jeb Cameron. In the end, it's always the women who have to do what needs doing."

"Your bitter tongue won't change what's right," Pa growled. "I'm going hunting."

He was out the door in two paces, rifle in hand. Mama slammed the door shut behind him. Jasper bolted off the porch.

I held my ground. Papa stopped when he saw me, worked his mouth some, blew out a short breath. "It'll smooth over," he told me. Then he stamped down the steps and started across the yard.

I ran after him. "Wait!"

He turned, the anger already draining from his face. "If you heard me speak my mind, there's no need to say it again."

"But—but Pa," I stammered. "We can't manage!"

He faced me with feet fixed firm, arms folded, eyes watchful but calm—just as he stood when facing a new field that needed clearing, or a bear after our livestock, or a fierce storm blowing over the ridge. "Hush now, Hannah. You may look like a girl, but I know you too well. You're stubborn as a mule. You'll help see things through. I wouldn't go off if I didn't believe that. You'll manage fine. I'm leaning on you."

"But why do you have to go?" The ache in my chest turned hot and started to smolder like banked coals.

"I'm for the Union," he said. "It's like a family. A clan. Sometimes people have to make sacrifices to hold the family together." He said more things too, but I stopped hearing the words. After a minute he ran a rough hand over my head, then tromped off.

I dragged back to the cornfield. Jasper, eyes shiny, wrestled a stone from the ground and heaved it onto the rock sled. He was skinny as a whittled stick, just nine years old but already game for hard work. And a good thing for that, I thought as I wrapped my fingers around a rock and pried it free. The dirt felt damp and cool against my skin. A vireo twittered from the walnut tree, but all I could hear was the echo of Pa and Mama's arguing. They most often spoke in silence: a thoughtful nod, a mouth hinting at a smile, a long shared glance. I'd never before heard them heave up ugly words from some dark cold place to throw at each other.

The earth smelled raw. The mountain murmured of new life, of plowing and planting, but everything had turned upside down. I heaved a rock at the sled—missed. Heaved another. Missed again. I wished Pa would come back. Then I might find my aim.

"Mind the sled!" Jasper complained, blinking hard.

I might have kept on wasting time if a familiar whistle hadn't startled a chickadee from its song. I sucked in a fierce, glad breath as Ben McNeill came round the doghobble thicket by the hog pen, a fishing pole over his shoulder.

"You got nothing better to do with your time than whistle?" I asked, when I could wrap my tongue around the words. On a normal day I took a fierce joy in any tune, but not today.

Ben grinned and followed a furrow until he stood at my shoulder. We were the same height. I liked that. I liked the way his dark hair curled around his ears when the air grew damp. I liked how his mind tended toward curiosity.

"That's a fine greeting for someone who came to bide some time," Ben said. Then he cocked his head, his eyes going narrow as he studied first me, then Jasper. But all he said was, "You want some help?"

"We'd be grateful," I allowed, and he tossed his pole aside. The McNeills were our closest neighbors, and good ones—the kind to share chores with, like husking and hog butchering. I didn't dare go fishing with Ben, not with Pa and Mama simmering. But Ben made any work lighter.

I'd known Ben for all thirteen of my years. Summers we fished for trout and madtoms and darters in Sandy Spring, and tried to figure out where the salamanders went when the cold bore down. Come autumn, we borrowed our papas' rifles and ranged the hills for turkey and wondered why they didn't grow head feathers. In winter, long after nutting season, we'd search for white-bellied mice nests in hollow trees, and wonder how they knew to hide away only chestnuts that weren't wormy. They even knew to eat the tiny heart from each nut so they didn't sprout when the weather got warm and damp. We never could figure that out.

Ben dragged the laden sled to the side of the corn patch and dumped the stones where they couldn't nick a plow blade. "Pa's fixing to leave," I said, when he'd dragged the empty sled back. "He's joining up with the Union Army."

Ben gave me another long look, chewing that news over before getting on with the job. He could talk my ear off, but he knew when to hold his tongue and give a body time.

I dropped a couple of stones on the sled. "Your pa heading off too?"

"Not so far as I've heard."

"I wish I was going somewhere too," Jasper said suddenly. "I wish it like anything."

A new vine of fear twined around my heart. "You're needed here!"

Jasper scowled. "I don't care. I want to go places like Papa. I'm sick and tired of Cumberland Mountain. I've had my fill of hoeing corn and chopping tobacco and picking rocks."

I crossed my arms. "Jasper Cameron, if you think we aren't staring at enough trouble—"

"Me, I like picking rocks," Ben said. He studied the rock in his hands as if it were a rare thing. "This came from the heart of Cumberland Mountain."

I'd never thought about it quite like that.

Ben shook his head in admiration. "Don't you ever wonder where these stones come from?"

"They rise up when the ground freezes and thaws, just to devil us," Jasper said sourly. "Everybody knows that."

"But how deep do they start?" Ben asked. "What fills the holes they leave behind? If enough years went by, would this mountain run out of rocks to keep shoving our way? Does it keep making more?"

"You might find out if you got off this mountain," Jasper pointed out. "There are bigger schools down in the flatlands."

Ben shrugged. "I figure all the answers I need are right here."

The hot coals of worry and anger I'd banked inside my chest started to fade some.

Ben stepped into the next row, crouched, and came back with an oval stone about the size of a bread loaf. "Here," he said, dumping it into my hands. "This is a fine one."

I stared at the heavy stone. It was gray like a dappled mare—as if all the grays of twilight had sunk into the ground and formed together and popped out again. "It *is* a fine one."

"You two are daft," Jasper snorted. But his eyes weren't tear-bright anymore.

"It would make a first-rate hearthstone," Ben added, and then went back to work.

Mama's words rang in my head: I'll *guard this hearth*. I'll *hold this family together*. A seed of something good planted itself in my heart.

Ben and Jasper and I spent the rest of the afternoon clearing the corn patch. Later, I hauled that dappled rock into the woods and left it cradled in the roots of my favorite old oak tree, safe till I might need it.

CHAPTER 1

I only heard my sweet mama cuss once. The Lord and I knew, even if my pa didn't, that she had good cause during those first two years of war. But she held out till the sticky-sweat day the Yankees came in 1863.

I stood in the doorway, looking in on Maude and Mary. When they were babies they'd sleep sucking each other's thumbs. Even now, they curled up together so tight when napping that it was hard to see where one left off and the next began.

"Can I have a drink?" Jasper asked behind me. I'd been washing grit from mustard greens and I heard him slosh the dipper in the bucket. Then his breath sucked in. *"Soldiers!"*

I whirled as the first of 'em came out from the trees to the tune of tramping feet and jingling tin cups and creaking leather haversacks. The soldiers carried their guns over their blue-coated shoulders, so the whole column bristled like teeth on a harrow. The endless column spilled from the trees and tromped past and on around the bend on the lane that dribbles in front of our farm, heading west.

Heading west. Toward the McNeill place. I pressed a hand beneath my ribs. *Ben* . . .

Jasper ran down to the road. I followed more slowly, with something like a big spider skittering down my backbone. These men must have been marching a long time. They'd come from the North. Jasper, who was partial to maps, probably knew where the North was. I just knew it was far. Beyond Cumberland Mountain, and beyond the Cumberland Gap into Kentucky.

The Yankee soldiers looked like they'd spent a long July day wrestling stumps from a new-gained field. My gaze lit on a gangly redhead not much older than Ben. His wool coat hung on him, the yellow plaid shirt underneath stained dark with sweat. His head hung lower than a thirsty dog's. Every step scuffed a cloud of dust, like he was too done in to pick his feet up. As he drew close I could see his cheeks were almost as red as his hair. He looked ready to go down of sunstroke.

I was about to haul that boy out of line for a dipper of water when I heard something else. My mama had left her hoe amongst the potato plants and come running to the rise at the field's edge. "Give 'em hell for East Tennessee!" she hollered. Her voice came out screechy as a rusty hinge.

My mouth dropped open. I waited for the hand of God to strike down from the heavens.

"*Hannah!*" Jasper gasped. "Mama—"

"Hush." I dug my fingers into his bony shoulder.

That redhead soldier grinned, and stepped livelier, and suddenly didn't look like he had one foot in the grave after all.

"Thanks from the Indiana boys!" he yelled. Some of the men cheered my mama, and waved.

She pulled off her apron and waved it back, calling over and over again. "Give 'em hell for East Tennessee!" She had a look on her face I'd never seen. Like she was willing to dare the wrath of our Rebel neighbors—even God Himself—to cheer those soldiers on. I stared, my skin still prickling. We watched until the column had finally shuffled past.

When the last soldier disappeared, Mama stood still. The tramping sound faded. A mourning dove called from the walnut tree by the cabin. Then Mama sagged, like the water yoke with two full buckets had dropped on her shoulders. She pressed one hand against her chest.

I hurried to her. "Jasper," I called sharply. "Get Mama a drink."

She turned to me slowly, mumbling.

"I didn't hear, Mama."

She swallowed hard. "I—I've tried to protect our hearth. Tried to hold this family together."

"You have done that, Mama."

Her fingers pressed into my arm. "It might be that I'll be needing your help on those counts, Hannah-girl."

Hadn't I been helping all this time? I hadn't set foot in school since Pa left so I could pitch in more at home.

Jasper hurried back with a tin cup sloshing water over the sides. Mama drained it dry and handed it to me. "Come with me, Jasper," she said. "Potatoes need hilling."

The spider feeling was still spooking up my backbone.

"Mama, can I run quick over to the McNeill place? I just want to see . . ." My voice trailed away. I hadn't spoken to Ben in over a year. At least not out loud, not face-to-face.

Mama fixed me with a stern look. "You know better than to ask such a thing." She began rubbing her left arm like it pained her. "Any trouble there is no business of ours. I need you to get those greens up. And check on the girls."

She had a gray look about her that reminded me of what mattered most. "Yes, Mama."

Mama quit rubbing her arm and tied her apron back on like it was a terrible chore. She didn't look defiant anymore. She looked worn down and tired. Tears had tracked through the dust on her cheeks. Guilt chewed at my belly as I turned back to our cabin.

The twins were only five, not much bigger than crickets, and Maude in particular feared strangers. I found Mary still asleep, sweet and peaceful. Maude sat beside her sister, arranging a collection of dried seedpods in rows on the quilt, singing a tuneless lullaby with words I didn't know.

"Maude!" I shook my head at her. "Sing in proper words the rest of us understand."

Maude stared at me, mouth tight in a frown, before silently going back to her game. I stepped back outside and realized Jasper had followed me. "Jasper! You better get on!"

"I will. But Hannah?" He squinted up at me. "Those Yankees were headed toward the McNeill place. What do you think's going to happen there?"

"I don't know."

"Trouble, do you think?"

"I said I don't know!" I snapped, then clamped my mouth closed tight.

I had never seen a true Yankee soldier before, unless you count my pa. That spring of 1861, he'd said his good-byes quick. One day he finished planting corn. That night he saw the new lambs slick-slide safe into the world. Next morning he tromped off to the war with a few other Union men. A few weeks later Tennessee voters approved the notion of leaving the Union and joining the new Confederacy. But a lot of men in the hills of East Tennessee were too stubborn to let the governor tell them what to do, and another bunch slipped away to join the Union Army.

Ben McNeill's pa didn't go with them. He waited a week or so before lighting out to join the Confederate Army with the other men too stubborn to let the North tell them what to do. Best I knew, Mr. McNeill was still alive, at least. Best I knew, Ben hadn't gotten the kind of letter we got four months after Pa left home, saying he'd been killed.

I stared down the road. "You go help Mama," I told Jasper. "There won't be any trouble at the McNeills'. That's Papa's army marching past. The Yankees aren't like the Confederates. They didn't come to trouble women and young folks."

Jasper and Mama spent the rest of the afternoon mounding earth around the potato plants. I pounded hominy and stitched the newest tear in Jasper's spare shirt. It was hard to think straight, though. The Yankees had come! Had they run all the Confederates out of East Tennessee? Middle Tennessee had been in Yankee hands for some time. We knew that because our aunt Ellen lived in Nashville, and had written us a letter. Were we safe now, like Papa had promised, or were the soldiers just firing up for a fight?

That night I boiled beans and greens for supper and waited for Mama to say something about the soldiers. She never did.

When the sun started to sink, I climbed up to the loft after the little ones. The little routines sat strange that night. I watched Jasper rub the little soldier Pa had carved for him, and wondered how those Yankees we'd seen were faring just now. Maude wandered beside a low beam, touching each of her most special treasures—a pretty pinecone, a spare bone button, a hen Pa had carved—and I saw the Yankees marching in file.

Mary sat watching, waiting for Maude to come to bed. People always said, "Those two are like as lima beans," but they weren't. Mary had squeezed into this world a good hour before Maude, born sickly, and still stood a shiver smaller than Maude. Maude was stronger, and looked out for Mary with a sharp eye. But Mary was wise, somehow, and she took Maude in hand from time to time.

Most of the time they didn't need me at all, but this was our special time. "Come here," I called when Maude was finished. They tumbled down beside me, one on each side, and Mary handed me a comb. I'd started combing their hair each night back before they were old enough to do it for each other, and I'd clung to that job. Mary couldn't abide hair in her face and was always glad to get a nice new braid.

Maude didn't care a whit about her hair, but she came too. "Hannah, sing!" she commanded.

My fingers wove Mary's fine hair into a skinny braid and tied it off with a strip of cloth. "What shall I sing?"

"You know!" she accused, then nestled up close.

One day, I thought, I might get tired of singing this song. But that day hadn't come yet, and I let my voice draw a warm blanket around us.

"As I walked out one evening fair
Out of sight of land,
There I saw a mermaid a-sitting on a rock
With a comb and a glass in her hand."

Mama climbed up to the loft with us after I'd sung all the verses. "Time for prayers now." She poked a bit of cotton stuffing back into a tired quilt before tucking it over the twins' shoulders. "And don't forget your papa."

"Why does Papa need our prayers, now that he's already dead and in heaven?" I asked.

She stared at me so long I wished I'd held my tongue. But finally she touched my cheek with one rough finger. "Pray so you always remember, Hannah. Remembering family gives a comfort, and can 'mind you that you have a place in this world."

After Mama heard our prayers, she slowly disappeared back down the ladder. The young ones fell asleep right away, huddled together like puppies to keep away the chill. I smelled a curl of tobacco as Mama lit her pipe. Sometime later, as full darkness came, I heard a puncheon floorboard creak before she slid into bed downstairs.

Maybe, I thought at last, the troubles will end now. The only men we'd seen in uniform so far were Confederates in butternut and gray. Rebels, those men called themselves, with more than a hitch of pride. They hadn't taken kindly to the fact that my papa fought to preserve the Union—

A muffled drumming jerked me up—horse hooves, pounding down our road. A horse shrilled like its rider had pulled up too hard, right in front of our cabin. I clutched the quilt, wishing I could tear away the darkness.

Half a dozen shots fired. Window glass shattered. Maude and Mary screamed like panthers, and Jasper woke with a holler. I screamed too, my heart thudding like a flail on wheat.

Just as quick, the night grew still. "Mama?" I called. I put my arms around the girls, trying to quiet their shakes. "Mama!"

"Hannah?" Jasper whimpered. "What happened?" His fingers clawed at my arm.

"Bushwhackers, most likely." They'd visited before—local men who didn't hold with my family's politics.

"We need to hide!" Mary shook my arm.

I took a deep breath, trying to suck courage in with the air. I wanted to pull the quilt over my head and wait for dawn to creep over the ridge, sweeping away the cabin's shadows like Mama swept away cobwebs. "Stay here," I whispered. "I need to see to Mama first."

I felt the grain of the hewn rungs under my bare feet like I'd never climbed down before. Every creak set my teeth on edge. "Mama?" I called again. No answer.

The air held an echo of tobacco smoke, and the mint I'd

hung to dry near the hearth, and something like an unemptied chamber pot. We'd banked the hearth coals good before going to bed, and the night sky had just a quarter moon. Mama's bed corner was solid black.

"Hannah?" Jasper called. I could tell he was about to cry. "What's wrong with Mama?"

"I don't know!" My voice cracked. My skin began to feel like the underbelly of a red-eared salamander, damp and cool. "Just wait."

We'd saved one candle for trouble, but it took me nigh on forever fumbling in the dark to find it. I stepped on a piece of glass, and pain stabbed through my heel. All the time I kept begging Mama to answer. *Please, Mama. Please.*

When I finally got that candle lit, I tiptoed to my mama's bed. She lay on her back, the old bear-tracks quilt tucked up to her chin. Her eyes were closed. I ripped back the quilt to see if one of those bullets had found her. She hadn't been shot, though. There was no blood. No sign of trouble. I put a hand on her shoulder and shook her. Again, harder. "Mama, wake up!"

But inside, I knew she couldn't wake up. I just *knew.*

Her heart must have purely quit. Maybe she took fright from the bushwhackers. Maybe it was the sight of the Yankees, finally come to bring the liberation my papa had promised. Or maybe it was the shock of hearing herself cuss.

But the cause didn't much matter. Mama was dead. Papa was dead. I had nothing left of Ben but a hole inside. I was alone in the world, with Mary and Maude and Jasper to tend.

I ended up on my knees beside the bed. I stroked Mama's

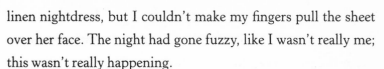

linen nightdress, but I couldn't make my fingers pull the sheet over her face. The night had gone fuzzy, like I wasn't really me; this wasn't really happening.

"Hannah!" Jasper's voice from the loft was shrill.

I clenched my teeth to keep from shrieking like a hawk-caught rabbit. After some time I folded Mama's arms gently across her chest like I'd seen other folks do with their dead, and smoothed every last wrinkle from the bedsheets.

"Hannah?" Mary this time, scared but quiet. I think she already knew.

I stole one last moment for me and Mama. I couldn't run off to cry like I had when we got the word about Pa. Not this time. My hurt got bundled up red and raw, and shoved down inside. "Good-bye, Mama," I whispered, and let her go. I had to.

I held the candle high and stumbled back up the ladder. "Mama's gone," I said, as gentle as I could, tears scorching my eyes. "She looks real peaceful, though. She didn't suffer."

Jasper began to cry in big snuffling gulps. Maude's eyes got big and glassy, and Mary clutched her hand. I pulled them all into my arms best I could, saying "Don't worry. I'm going to take care of you," over and over so none of them had space to say "How, Hannah? How are you going to do that?"

Finally my voice dribbled away. I felt soft little fingers patting the back of my hand. "Shouldn't we hide?" Mary asked again.

"Yes." I forced myself to think of this moment, nothing else. "Those bushwhackers might come back. Grab your clothes."

I helped the girls pull on their dresses quick as I could, and had Jasper bring our quilts. I was afraid the cabin might get burned down. News that the Yankee soldiers had finally come was likely to bring out the worst hatred of our Rebel neighbors. *Ben . . .*

We'd seen some ugly things since Papa left. Neighbors, old friends, had sent Rebel men to steal from us. After it happened once, Mama told me to take Jasper and the girls to the woods at the first sign of trouble. "Watch over the young ones," she told me, real fierce. "No matter what comes." The next time it happened I took the little ones down behind the ridge. We saw smoke pluming to the heavens, and only the memory of the look in Mama's eyes when she ordered me to tend the children had kept me from running back to her. When we finally stole home at dusk we found the pig shed burned to the ground, and the smokehouse too.

The next time we hid from the bushwhackers, shadows were long by the time we crept home. Mama was sitting silent in her rocking chair by the hearth. The fire was down to embers, so first thing I laid a few sticks of kindling on the coals and blew flames to life.

"You hurt, Mama?" I asked. I felt a mighty stillness in the cabin, poised and watchful, ready to pounce. The kids lined up silent against the wall, all owl-eyes. I heard a crackle as one of the hickory sticks caught. The shadows shifted and sighed.

And then I saw. "Oh, *Mama,*" I breathed. I knelt beside her chair and reached toward her face—toward the pork-chop-size bruise on her cheek, the crust of blood on her lip, the eye swollen shut. My fingers fluttered like moths, afraid to light on all that pain. I took her hand instead. After a bit her fingers squeezed mine, and she began to come back to us.

I felt my heart break that evening, just break like a robin's sweet blue egg. It broke for Mama, and for the little ones, and for my foolish dead pa. But most of all it had broken for me and Ben. I'd known down deep—deep as the heart of Cumberland Mountain—that nothing would ever be the same.

And I was right, I thought, leading the younger ones down the ladder.

"Watch the broken glass," I said. My own foot was sticky with blood. Once Jasper had gotten clear, I snuffed the candle and we felt our way outside. Jasper was still sniffling and scrubbing his eyes, and I led the way back around the corn patch and into the woods. Once we were settled a safe distance away, behind the reassuring bulk of my old oak tree, I touched his arm. "Go get Star," I whispered.

"You go!"

Maude tightened her grip, clinging like a wood tick. I pressed my cheek against her hair, fiercely glad to feel needed. "I can't manage the twins and the mule. Go!" I ordered in a hoarse, trembling whisper.

It seemed like forever before Jasper crept back with Star and staked her to a shagbark hickory. That mule had pulled my family's plow for as long as I could remember. Star was about all we had left. "Good job, Jasper."

I heard him wipe his nose on his sleeve. "I wish Pa were here." His voice shook.

"Well, he's not!" I hissed. "He left us, and now see what's happened."

Jasper didn't answer. After a minute I swallowed hard and put my arm around his shoulders. Maude and Mary began whispering together in their secret language, and for once, I let them hide in their own place. Hearing every rustle, I wondered if the bushwhackers were coming back.

And I thought about Mama. Pa's people were what they call Scots-Irish and had deep roots in Tennessee, but Mama's parents had arrived straight from Scotland. On snowy evenings she'd sometimes sit by the hearth and tell stories that made our smoky cabin walls fade to the heather of a Scottish glen. Every once in a while she'd let us sleep past first light, and I'd wake with my mouth already juicing up, the smell of wheat cakes and curdled milk climbing to the loft. "Face the morning," she'd call up the ladder. "I've got flannel cakes and bonnyclabber waiting. . . ."

I'd never taste Mama's flannel cakes again.

Jasper snuffled again. "Jasper?" I whispered. "Scootch closer by me. You can lean against my shoulder and try to sleep."

"I'm not going to sleep!" he protested. But he scootched closer anyway.

I hitched back so I could lean against the oak tree. My fingers brushed against a stone. *My* stone. I squeezed the rock until my fingers hurt, remembering the day Ben had helped Jasper and me pick new spring rocks. I remembered further back, to the day Ben taught me to skip stones on the pool at Sandy Spring that summer. "Let's do a double," he'd cried once I'd got the hang of it, and we each danced a stone across the water, trying to see whose would go the farthest.

And I remembered hearing him hiss my name, on a blue-sky, goose-flight autumn morning the year my pa left. I'd been picking corn, and he waited in the thicket near field's edge till I got close. "I had to see you, Hannah," he said. "We can't let all this trouble come between us. Your pa gone Union Army, and my pa gone Confederate. We can't let them tell us not to be friends. I'm going hunting tomorrow noon. Meet me at Sandy Spring? Promise?" Hidden by the whispering cornstalks, I'd nodded. He crept away and I went back to work, sure Ben and I could do better than the elders all around us, letting war rip them apart.

But that afternoon the bushwhackers came and hurt my mama. The war became rage and terror and a cruel hard meanness that sliced into my family like a meat ax. The next day I looked hard at Mama's face. Come noon I marched straight down to Sandy Spring. I planted my feet and folded my arms and faced Ben down: "Your people beat my mama yesterday, Ben McNeill—"

"What?"

"—and I'll be your friend again the day you turn your back on the Confederacy. Not one minute before."

Ben's mouth worked like a landed trout. "But—but Hannah—"

"Don't you 'But Hannah' me!" I snapped. "We Camerons know the difference between right and wrong." I'd turned my back on the stunned look in his dark eyes, still so angry that tears spilled over all the way back home.

I wished for that anger now. That forever night, my legs twitched with wanting to creep through the brush to Ben's place. I almost did. Then I thought again of those bushwhackers shooting in our windows—men who shared the same politics as Ben's family.

The bushwhackers didn't come back. But it was a long night.

CHAPTER 2

At first light I sent Jasper to the nearest Union neighbor for help. The Duncans lived across the next hollow and up the creek, almost two miles away. "You wait on the porch, and I'll fetch some corn cakes," I told the girls.

Once inside, I ended up standing by Mama's bed instead of looking for food. The lump in my throat got so big I thought I just might choke and end up laid out too. For a moment, that filled me with a mighty longing. Then Maude started whimpering. A fly started in buzzing near Mama. I wiped my eyes and smashed that fly good, right against the wall.

After I fed the girls, I took a grub hoe to the garden. "What do you want us to do?" Mary asked. They were sticking to me like shadows.

"Check the squash vines for worms," I told them. We couldn't afford to lose a single plant. Mary set to work. Maude wandered along behind.

I attacked the weeds like bushwhackers. We can't do it alone, my mind said with every slice. We have to, my heart answered. I looked ahead at the plowing and harrowing and cooking and corn picking, with nothing but a tired mule and three skinny kids for help. We'd barely gotten by as it was, since Papa had gone off to war, and that was with Mama working herself to a nub. And for a while we'd had a cow and chickens and hogs too, before the bushwhackers got them—

Maude yanked on my skirt. "Hannah!"

"What?" I paused, wiping sweat from my forehead. She pointed to a plume of smoke rising above the treetops to the west. It grew until big rolls of smoke boiled toward the sky.

I squeezed the hoe like to snap it in two. "It's from the McNeill place."

Then I heard Jasper shout. When I saw the neighbor following him from the trees I wanted to weep with relief. Mrs. Duncan was a tall gray-haired woman who could set a broken bone or feed fifteen men at a barn raising or shoot a panther troubling her cow.

She marched right through the corn patch to greet us. "You poor girls," she said, smoothing Maude's hair. "Your blessed mother's gone to her reward. My husband's off to fetch Preacher and his wife, and the O'Briens too."

I pointed out the smoke staining the western sky. "There's trouble at the McNeill place," she agreed, squinting. "It's of no mind to us, though. Anyone bothering those Rebels will be leaving us alone. Come inside."

As she shooed the twins inside I stared west again. The old ache stitched itself right to my heart, pounding with each billow of smoke. *We can't let them tell us not to be friends. . . .*

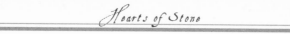

Then I thought about Mama, turned my back, and marched into the cabin. My cabin now. *My* hearth.

Mrs. Duncan made a pot of sassafras tea and poured us each a mug with a big dollop of honey in it. Then she helped me lay Mama out in her best dress. "I wish we had finer," I said, fingering a tear in the skirt of Mama's brown polished cotton.

"Her soul's already with the Lord, and the Lord don't mind such things. Here, now. You want me to put her ring away safe for you?"

The wedding ring on Mama's finger—a circle of gold with a green stone in the center—was a rare fine thing. Papa's mama had worn it, and his grandmother too. Maybe more, no one was sure. "No," I said. "I want it."

Mrs. Duncan frowned to see how loose the ring was on my skinny finger. "You're going to lose it. Let me put it away safe until you're grown."

"No." I found a good piece of string on the shelf where Mama kept spare bits of twine and such, looped it through the ring, and knotted it behind my neck.

By the time Mrs. Duncan was finished, Alta and Matthew O'Brien came with their baby, and Preacher Peabody and his wife with all their children. Mr. Peabody was a big man who preached a fiery Gospel and raised the best bear-hunting dogs in four counties. "You children mustn't mourn your mother," he said. "She has gone on from this world of woe."

True enough. I just wished she hadn't left us behind to face the world of woe alone.

The men scratched a grave from the stubborn soil. I helped

wrap Mama in a blue wool blanket, and we laid her to rest best we could. Preacher Peabody recited quite a spell from the Good Book. "Ezekiel 36:26," he boomed, shooting a look at Alta as the baby on her shoulder began to squall. "A new heart also will I give you, and a new spirit will I put within you; and I will take away the stony heart out of your flesh. . . ."

A heart of stone. That's what I needed. Then I wouldn't feel the brambles still twining around my heart, or the leftover Ben-ache. My eyes felt sandy. I could hardly swallow. I tried to pay attention, truly. But my gaze strayed toward the western sky. The smoke was gone.

I surely wished Ben and his hadn't gone for the Confederacy, and we could have invited them to the burial. It used to be that Mama and Mrs. McNeill turned to each other in times of need, and helped out in times of sorrow. It used to be that Ben and I—

"Amen," Preacher thundered.

He turned away. I crouched and laid one palm on the rocky mound. "Good-bye, Mama," I whispered. "I'll do the best I can." Then I followed the rest back inside.

Mrs. Duncan fixed more tea, and Alta unwrapped a loaf of rye bread she'd brought. She was just a year or so older than me, new-married, but the older women accepted her as one of their own. I watched her rough hands as they sliced the bread, quick and even, and imagined her tending her own hearth. Was it just that extra year she had on me that made her so certain? Or did her calm come from Matthew's quiet gaze, and the knowing that she needn't defend her hearth alone? I had to look away. Then I noticed Jasper and the girls gobbling the meal, licking their fingers, and felt my fear march back inside. I slid my own piece into my pocket. We'd have it for supper.

When we had finished, Mrs. Duncan shooed us back out-side like geese. "You young ones go on outside for a spell. Let your elders talk for a bit." I glanced at Alta, wanting to stay, but she had gone to stand by her Matthew. I could almost hear Mama: *Mind your elders, Hannah.* So we went.

We were all hoeing and pitching rocks in the corn patch when Mrs. Duncan called. The twins and Jasper followed me in. The neighbor kids kept on chopping weeds.

Something in the air made me uneasy as soon as I stepped into the cabin. Mrs. Duncan folded her arms and took charge. "We've worked some things out."

I licked my lips. "About what?"

Preacher Peabody frowned. "About you children, Hannah. You can't stay here alone, now that your mother has passed on."

I went still as stone.

"Have you any kin nearby?" Alta asked kindly.

"Just my mother's sister Ellen, in Nashville."

Mrs. Duncan gave Alta a satisfied look. "Just as I said."

"Nashville is two hundred miles away," Preacher Peabody said. "That's no help. Hannah, you will come to live with me. Mrs. Peabody can use a good strong girl like you to help with the chores."

Something began to pound in my brain.

Preacher looked at my brother. "Jasper, the Duncans are

willing to let you live with them. You'll have to work hard, earn your keep."

Jasper stared at me with wide eyes.

"As for the twins, the O'Briens have kindly agreed to take them in." Preacher Peabody cleared his throat. "It's a generous offer, since they'll eat more than they'll earn for a time to come."

Mary went very still, drawing into herself. Maude buried her face in my skirt. I could feel her trembling. "No!" I burst out, putting one hand on her shoulder while I struggled to find words. The blackberry vines threatened to choke my heart altogether. "It's a kindly offer," I managed finally. "And we're grateful. But . . . we'd like to stay together."

Mrs. Duncan nodded. "I understand, child. But none of us can take on four more mouths to feed."

"We'd work real hard!" Jasper said anxiously. "And we wouldn't eat much. I promise."

Preacher Peabody shifted his weight, and the chair groaned in protest. "It's a burden as it is. Especially the twins—"

"We don't mind a bit," Alta said quickly. "We'll manage." I saw sadness in her eyes, but guilt too. "We wish we could do as you want, Hannah," she added. Matthew studied his hands.

"You'll still see each other," Mrs. Duncan added. "We're not spread so far as that."

No . . . but far enough. Since the troubles had started, folks mostly stayed close to home. Even Preacher spent more time coaxing corn out of the ground than spreading the Gospel.

I firmed up my voice. "Well, we'll just stay on here, then. We can manage."

Mr. Duncan frowned. "How can you get your crops tended and harvested, all the while cooking and cleaning? And worrying about the bushwhackers the whole time?"

"I think we can do it," I lied.

"I won't leave four children on their own." Preacher drummed big fingers on the table. "It's not Christian. You'll do as we've said, and be grateful you have a roof over your heads."

The room was quiet. Maude wrapped her arms around my legs. I looked out the window toward that fresh grave. "We're grateful," I said again, flashing Jasper a fierce look: *Hold your tongue for now.* "But we'd like to stay here tonight—"

"It's not safe, child," Mr. Duncan said.

"Just to get our things together," I pressed on. "We'll be all right. It can't be any worse than last night. I want to spend one more night here."

Preacher looked unhappy. Mrs. Duncan began to shake her head. Then Alta nodded. "If Hannah wants to spend a last night here, we should let her. She probably wants to say good-bye to her mother."

"Yes, thank you," I said quickly.

The neighbors headed home. I watched them disappear among the trees and wanted to weep with relief. I'd bought one night to figure out a plan.

Inside, we sat at the table. Jasper sank his face in his hands. Mary laid her head on her arms. Maude twined her fingers into my skirt. For a while no one said anything. Finally Jasper looked up at me with pleading eyes. "Hannah, I don't want to go live with the Duncans. I know they're good folks. But—"

"I know."

"I think we can make it on our own," Jasper said earnestly. "I'll work really hard, Hannah. Harder than before. We can do it."

"I want to believe that," I said slowly, staring at my knuckles. "I do. But I just don't think . . ." I rubbed my forehead with my fingers.

"I want to stay with you, Hannah," Maude whispered.

"I know." I gently pulled free of Maude, stepped to the fireplace, and picked up a battered photograph. Before Papa left home a traveling photographer had come to Walnut Cove during a religious meeting, with a pretty bay horse pulling the funny wagon where he kept his camera and fixings, and we'd all gone and sat for him. Papa scrubbed up, and slicked his hair back neat. Mama stared like the camera was the devil's own contraption. I stuck my arms behind my back because the sleeves on my best dress were too short, and I didn't want my scrawny arms captured for all eternity. Jasper managed to have a piece of hair sticking straight up in back. And Maude and Mary were little more than a blur. It wasn't much of a photograph, I guess, but Pa had carried it off to war. The officer who wrote the bad news about Pa sent it back.

When I put the likeness back I ran my fingers over the stones above the mantel. Mama had helped Pa build this hearth before I was born, with stones from the heart of Cumberland Mountain. Somehow she broke her only china plate during those days, and Pa plastered a shard of it—white, with pretty red flowers— right into the chimney to ease her heart.

A new thought slid into my head, hopeful and hard. I had to choose.

I took a deep breath, then let the words crawl out. "I . . . have . . . an idea."

"What?" Jasper asked eagerly.

"How about we go to Nashville and find Aunt Ellen?"

Jasper frowned. "Aunt Ellen?"

I sat down again. "Do you remember her?"

"A bit." He scrunched his forehead. "She looked like Mama."

"Yes. Like Mama." I looked at the girls. "Aunt Ellen used to come visit us sometimes. Before the war." In my mind I saw Mama looking years younger as she and her sister laughed together over the laundry kettle. I heard them singing love songs in time to the butter churn. I felt the feather of Aunt Ellen's finger touching my cheek, just as Mama's sometimes did. . . . My throat burned, and I swiped at my eyes. "She's family."

"Nashville is a long way," Jasper said slowly.

"I think we can make it." I was sorting it through. "We can hitch Star to the cart, and pack some of our things. We'll have to walk—she's too worn out to carry our weight too. But Maude and Mary can ride sometimes."

"What about the war?" Jasper asked. "Suppose we head out and run smack-dab into it?"

"We could run into trouble," I allowed. "But we've got trouble right here too. Those bushwhackers could hit Preacher's place, or one of the others, easy as they hit ours." I looked from face to face. "Well, what do you say? Shall we go find Aunt Ellen?"

The girls exchanged a heavy glance. Jasper chewed his lip. "I don't know," he said finally.

An ache of pure loneliness welled up inside. Had Papa felt this way when he decided to leave the family and join the Union Army? Had he felt this weight?

No. This was different. I was making a choice that would hold the family together, not one that would rip it apart. I shrugged Papa's memory aside angrily and tried again. "Do you want to get split up, or stay together?"

"Well . . . stay together," Jasper said, and Mary followed too: "Stay together." Maude nodded.

"Then we're heading to Nashville." I took a deep breath and sent a little prayer up to the sky: *Mama, I can't defend our hearth and keep the family together too. Am I choosing right?*

No answer.

We were on our own.

We packed up at first light.

I wanted to leave a letter for Mrs. Duncan, or Preacher, or whoever came by first to look for us. I didn't have any clean paper, so I used the back of the letter the army had sent about Papa getting himself killed.

I am fetching the children to Nashville to find our aunt Ellen. Hannah Cameron

I left the letter on the table, weighted with a stone. I wasn't worried that anyone would come after us. Our neighbors had done their Christian part, and no one had time or duty to chase us down the road.

Jasper hitched Star to the two-wheeled cart Papa had used to haul grain to Jacksboro. I tried to judge both what we'd need and what Star could pull. A pile of folded quilts. Mama's warm wool cloak, Jasper's coat, the girls' shawls. All the food I could find: a half-barrel of cornmeal, a little rice, a crock of old bacon grease, some dried fruit and beans, a basket of peas and carrots and onions. I tucked in our last candle, a bar of lye soap, a couple of dish towels, a skillet, matches, and four each of tin plates, spoons, and mugs. Finally, I hid away the little leather bag of coins Mama'd kept under her mattress. I wore my shoes, on account of my cut foot, but I slid everyone else's in the cart to save on wear.

Mary crouched in the dust, watching. When she sank into such stillness, I never knew if she was thinking, or just shoring up her strength. I swallowed hard and sent up a quick prayer.

Then Maude began making piles on the front porch: iron kettles, wool carding combs, flax hackles, candle molds. "Maude, *stop*," I burst out finally. "I told you, nothing but what we absolutely need. Help me haul this stuff back inside."

Once that was done she started up the loft ladder. "I've already got your things," I called.

Maude froze on a rung, looking from me to the loft. "My things are up there!" Tears pooled up and spilled over.

I clenched my fists. "Mary," I finally called. When she slid inside, I said, "Help me explain to Maude. We *can't* take everything."

I watched Mary sidle close to Maude and murmur something. Saw a whole conversation unfold in the long look they shared. I scrubbed another tear away and waited for them to work it out.

Mary finally turned to me. "Can we take Dolly?"

Relief sagged my shoulders. "For certain. She'll help you remember Mama." I touched Mama's wedding ring, hid beneath my bodice on its string.

Then I looked through the open door at Jasper, fussing with the cart. "Jasper? You want to take that soldier Pa carved for you?"

He shook his head, staring at the dirt and trying to look like a man.

I bit my lip, then nodded. Papa had sent a likeness of himself from the training camp where he learned soldiering. I remember staring at the image captured on a little piece of tin, trying to find my pa in that soldier standing stiff and stern in his new uniform. Ma kept it on the mantel, and when we got the family photograph back from the army, it joined the one of Pa, smack in the center.

I fetched the tintypes and stared at Pa for a moment, and tasted something bitter. "This is what comes of marching off to war," I muttered.

Then I fetched them outside. "Jasper, will you take charge of these?"

He grabbed them from my hand and slid them into his shirt pocket. "I guess," he said, with a big shrug. "I'll go fetch a bucket so we can water Star."

I patted the mule. Until Jasper grew big enough to help, I'd tended Star. "It's a fit chore for you, Hannah," Papa had said more than once. "You're as stubborn as the mule." But he always smiled when he said it.

"Are you up to the trip, Star?" I whispered. Poor girl. Her sides were furrowed as a new-plowed field. "You can get us to Nashville, can't you?" I scratched her between the ears, then took stock. Jasper'd come back with the bucket. The cart was packed. Mary and Maude stood waiting. Everything was ready.

My chest began to ache. "I forgot something," I said.

Jasper snorted. "Hannah—"

"Just hush up and wait!"

Back inside I touched the marks my fingers had made in the clay and straw chinked between the logs when we'd had to repair damage done by mice and bees and rain. I set Mama's rocking chair to motion so I could hear it creak. I trailed my hand over the oak table Papa had hewn, and toed the crack between the puncheons where Jasper always dropped his string beans through for the chickens. Jasper didn't much care for string beans.

"I can't protect the hearth, Mama," I whispered. I tried to pry the flowered china piece free of the chimney, but it stuck fast. I polished it with my apron instead.

Then my gaze lit on the family Bible, kept on its own little table near the fireplace. Like the wedding ring, it came across the ocean with my papa's family many years before. The huge book had a tooled-leather cover that was surely the envy of Preacher Peabody. Inside were special pages where generations of Camerons had written down births and weddings and deaths. That faded, spidery writing was all that was left of their lives.

The Bible rested on a square scrap of plaid wool, dark green and blue with thin yellow stripes, which had come across the ocean with Mama's parents.

I carried the Bible and the tartan cloth outside, wrapped them in a quilt, and stowed them in the cart. "Now we're ready," I said, putting a hand on Star to steady myself.

"Hannah?" Jasper chewed his lip. "What happens if we can't find Aunt Ellen in Nashville?"

"Well . . . we'll come back here. We can always go to the neighbors if need truly be."

"But what will happen to our place?"

I drew a deep breath. "Nothing, I hope. We own this land, legal. There are papers in Knoxville to prove it. When the war's over we'll come back and start again."

I took a last look around. The ash hopper beside the big boiling kettle was full, waiting for Mama to fire up a batch of laundry. The big iron hoisting hook still hung in the walnut tree by the pigpen, waiting for Papa to haul up a butchered pig to dress out. Corn was coming up in the field, and the garden needed tending, and a pile of ginseng waited on the porch. Two fresh 'coon skins were nailed on the front wall to dry.

And Mama's grave still fresh and bare.

I finally pried my gaze away and planted myself in the road. I folded my arms, staring west. "You look just like Pa," Jasper said.

That shored me up some. "I'll get us to Nashville," I promised. "Let's get going."

CHAPTER 3

I figured to get ten miles behind us before we stopped for the night. At that rate, we'd get to Nashville in three weeks. I could make our food last that long if I was careful.

But we hadn't gone half a mile from home when Star suddenly balked, tossing her head. "Hey there, girl!" Jasper cried, grabbing her halter.

Then my nose sniffed it too: a cold stink of stale smoke. Jasper jerked his head to look at me. "It's the McNeill place," he whispered. "What should we do?"

Each fine hair on the back of my neck rose. I had to swallow twice to get my tongue moving. "Maybe we can steal by without anybody noticing," I whispered back.

Jasper tugged Star's halter and led the way through the last fringe of trees. My hopes fell like windfall apples.

The stable stood by its lonesome in the McNeills' clearing. A blackened chimney marked the cabin's grave. A few charred beams poked skyward, as if asking for a second chance. Gray ash sifted and sighed on a puff of breeze.

"Oh Lordy," Jasper breathed. Maude and Mary stared.

I pinched my skirt into folds. "Maybe . . . maybe we should see if they need help."

As I took one step forward, Ben McNeill walked out of the stable, leading their mule. He stopped when he saw us. For the first time in over a year, my gaze found his. Ben's eyes were the same and different both—still knowing, but pooled with something deep and sad I'd never seen. Something quivered between us in the still morning. I raised my hand. He took one step.

Then Mrs. McNeill and her daughter, Sary, appeared. Mrs. McNeill carried a big bundle. Sary, who wasn't yet ten, had an oak-splint basket almost too big to haul. When Mrs. McNeill saw us she dropped her bundle and ran toward the road. "Yankee devils!" she shrieked. She stooped, then hurled a rock at us. "Get out of here!" Her first rock went wild, but the second bounced off the side of the cart.

Maude screamed. Star snorted and stamped.

I shoved the girls toward Jasper. "Keep them behind the cart! If need be, run for it." I grabbed Star's halter and tugged her toward the far side of the clearing.

Then Ben picked up a rock and hurled it. "Yankee devils!" he yelled. His rock bounced off the cart, but its shadow landed down in the Ben-hole beneath my ribs.

He and Sary and their mother howled those words over and over, crazed-like. Mrs. McNeill's hair straggled down in her face. A rock hit Star in the flank, and her leather harness burned into my palms as she tried to bolt. Ben threw a rock that hit me in the leg.

Finally we made it to the woods beyond. Ben ran a few steps into the road to hurl one final stone, but it sailed wide. The yells died away. Mrs. McNeill begin to wail instead.

I pushed on for a bit before daring to stop, numb as frostbite. "I don't think they're following us," I said, and Jasper nodded.

We rested for a few minutes in the shelter of a huge chestnut tree. Maude's sobs dwindled to messy sniffles, and Mary wiped her nose on her sleeve. "It's all right now, girls. I won't let anyone hurt you." I opened my mouth to sing a lullaby, but my ears were still full of Ben's curses and his mother's unearthly keening.

I'd never heard Mrs. McNeill screech like that, even when she once lost a baby to fever. We buried that babe on a cold day, beneath gray skies that made everyone feel worse. "I wish we never came here!" Mrs. McNeill had wept. "I wish my sisters were here. . . ."

"You're not alone," Mama had said firmly, with an arm around Mrs. McNeill's shoulders. "You hear me? We'll be your new family. Hear?" And Mrs. McNeill had finally nodded and let Mama lead her away from that tiny grave.

After the burying was done, Ben ran off. I found him down by Sandy Spring, sitting with legs drawn up and face hidden on his knees. I know he heard me come, but he didn't move. "Ben?" I put a hand on his arm.

"Don't!" he flared, twisting away. For a moment we both sat, both lost, with nothing but the water's burble for company. Then Ben began to sniffle. I put my hand on his shoulder. He jerked, but I squeezed and hung on. And Ben had cried then, with deep shuddering gasps that shook his whole body. We'd sat like that till he was cried out. Then I'd led him back to his own hearth, where friends had gathered with corn bread and venison stew.

Well, I knew the other side now. I knew that the next rain would turn the ashes of Ben's cabin heavy and sullen—just like the mound of ruin at our place, where our pig shed and smokehouse used to be. I knew that war could turn hearts the same way.

I caught Jasper's eye and nodded. "You did good, Jasper."

"Do you think it was the Yankee soldiers that burned their place?" he asked.

"Could be some mean soul feeling braver now that the Yankees have come to East Tennessee, and taking revenge for all the Rebel folks' ugliness."

"What kind of kin do the McNeills have?"

I watched Maude gathering twigs like flowers. "I don't know."

"I just thought—you and Ben being friends, and all . . ."

I shoved to my feet. "Ben's as dead to me as Mama. Come on. We've got a long way to go."

I tramped on with one ear cocked for the creak of the McNeills' mule cart, coming behind us. They'd likely be following the same trace we were, down toward bigger roads. I couldn't countenance the thought of seeing Ben McNeill just then, so I pushed hard. We stopped a few times to water Star, and paused to munch old corn cakes and dried apples when the sun stood high. Those mountain roads were narrow and steep. "Going up you

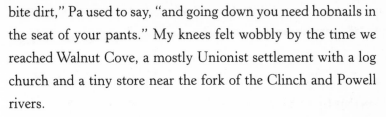

bite dirt," Pa used to say, "and going down you need hobnails in the seat of your pants." My knees felt wobbly by the time we reached Walnut Cove, a mostly Unionist settlement with a log church and a tiny store near the fork of the Clinch and Powell rivers.

I'd already given in and let the girls ride in the cart, but Jasper looked like lifting each foot was a powerful chore. Aside from one runny-nosed boy trotting past with a fishing pole, and a hound dog snoring in front of the store, I didn't see a soul. I stopped at the riverbank to let Star slurp greedily. "We'll take a quick rest," I said. "But not too long."

"I'm going into Hanson's," Jasper announced. "I want to look at the map." The storekeeper had a big map of the United States pinned on his wall.

I folded my arms. "What did I just say to you? You don't need—"

"We're setting out from home!" Jasper said stubbornly. "We should study the map!"

I let him go. Papa had once explained that map to me and Jasper, pointing and reading strange names. I couldn't make a bit of sense of all the squiggly lines and odd shapes, but something had sparked in Jasper's eyes.

The twins and I waited in the shade of an ancient sycamore. Mary fashioned a bright bonnet for Dolly from a big leaf. I looked back over my shoulder, up the trail, not even minding the girls' secret whispers. I didn't see Ben. I did see, in my mind, Pa and Ben's father, coming down that very trail each spring to gig catfish. They brought back fish weighing sixty or seventy pounds apiece, and baskets of mussels too. Mama and Mrs. McNeill would fry up that fish just right, so it fell from the bone and melted in our mouths like butter. In the cold months Ben and I'd pull stools close to one hearth or the other, and fashion buttons from the mussel shells—

"Hey, Hannah." Jasper padded across the trace and plopped down beside us. "I got it all fixed in my head. And here." He grubbed in his pocket. "Look! Four lemon drops!"

I stared like he'd pulled out spiders. "Jasper Cameron, you got stump water between your ears? We don't have money for lemon drops!"

"I used my Christmas penny," he said sulkily. "I got one for each of us."

Maude snatched her piece and popped it in her mouth. Mary looked at me sideways. I sighed and nodded; too late for anything else. "Thank you, Jasper," Mary said.

"Thank you," Maude chimed in. The tiny smile that touched the corners of her mouth made my heart twitch.

"See?" Jasper said to me accusingly.

"We can't afford that kind of foolishness." I shoved to my feet.

"You're an old sulk, Hannah Cameron." Jasper tossed a prickly seedball away, making a big show of sucking his lemon drop—and mine.

I looked back up the silent trace one more time. Nothing. Then I looked down the other way. I'd never been farther down this road than Walnut Cove before. I planted myself in the road, folded my arms, and stared it down.

———

We reached a clear stream as shadows stretched long. "This looks like a good spot," I said. "Let's make camp. You three fetch some firewood. I'll start supper." No one argued. Jasper'd worn a mule look ever since leaving Walnut Cove. He'd chop his hand off before admitting he was tired. But he looked about used up.

I'd only brought the one skillet to cook in, so I had to mix the cornmeal and water in one of our tin cups. "You planning to eat tonight or tomorrow?" Jasper asked, watching me stir with one finger.

"You hush your mouth. And start figuring how we're going to balance this skillet over the coals long enough to cook."

"Why didn't you bring the spider?" He meant the cast-iron skillet with three legs.

"Because it was too big and heavy. Go look by the creek for some good rocks."

He sighed like I'd asked him to carry back a kitchen stove. But soon enough he came back with half a dozen stones and dumped them on the ground. By that time the fire was burning well, and I had a dollop of grease waiting in the frypan. "We just need . . . oh, maybe three about the same size," I said, scrabbling through the pile, and picked up one I thought would suit.

I must have been plumb worn out, because when I picked it up, my eyes got blurry with tears.

After a minute we got the skillet balanced on three rocks and started frying corn cakes. The first batch burned when I shoved a stick of fat pine into the embers and flames flared up and caught the bacon grease on fire. I had to wait until the whole mess cooled down enough to scrub out in the creek and start over.

"For cripes' sake, Hannah," Jasper complained. He was slumped in the dirt nearby.

"Don't say another word!" I rounded on Jasper, blinking back more angry tears. "Do you think I don't hate this? I hate this war. I hate Ben. And I hate Pa!"

Jasper jerked like he'd been snakebit.

I turned away. Lord Almighty, I'd thought I knew what hatred was—like hating the sound of new calves bawling for their mothers, or the taste of gooseberries before they came full ripe, or how stupid I felt knowing that Jasper understood maps and I didn't. But those things—all those things before the war—were nothing compared to what I felt now.

Finally I took a deep, shuddery breath. Unclenched my fists. And managed to make our supper. "All right, now, on your feet," I said. We all stumbled stiffly to our feet and recited a prayer, and I almost heard my father's voice: "I believe my God prefers a man with self-respect enough to stand in His presence."

We spread our quilts on the ground and settled down. Maude handed me a yellow leaf. "Here, Hannah."

"This is for me? Thank you." I took her gift and rested my cheek on her head for a moment, sucking in her sweet scent. Then I stretched a hand toward Mary. "Fetch the comb." There beneath the trees I eased the tangles from the girls' hair and sang "The Mermaid," and watched the hard set to Jasper's mouth ease out as he lay nearby and listened.

Mama, if you can, watch over us. We've got a long way to go.

I kept the fire burning low to keep bear and bobcat and porcupines away, but the night was loud with buzzing and skittering, croaking and hooting, once even some howling off in the distance. It all made for a spooky choir, without a stout cabin wall between us, so I was still awake when a breeze picked up. I sniffed it unhappily—rain on the way. The first boom of thunder shuddered through.

"Don't mind. That's just the bread wagon," Mary mumbled, like Pa used to. He'd meant that thunder brought rain, which made our corn and wheat grow.

Well, it wouldn't do us a lick of good if our corn did grow. "Storm's coming." I sighed. "Let's crawl under the cart."

I fumbled in the dark for a little piece of oilcloth I'd brought and made sure it was tucked firm over the cornmeal and the Bible. Then I tried to hang some quilts over the wheels for a makeshift shelter before squeezing under the cart with the others. But the rain came down fierce, and the wind drove it sideways, and soon we were cold and wet and purely miserable.

"When we get to Aunt Ellen's, everything will be well again," I promised.

"Do you think so?" Jasper's voice came thin out of the gloom.

"Nashville is a big city. Why, I imagine Aunt Ellen lives in a nice big house. She'll likely fix a chicken dinner to welcome us. Chicken and dumplings."

"I'd rather have ham."

"Ham then. Ham and sweet potatoes and peas."

"Hannah, I'm cold," Maude whimpered.

"I know. We all are. Mary, scooch over closer." I wrapped my arms around her more tightly to help her shivers.

"I want to go home," she said. "Hannah, let's go home tomorrow."

"I th-think we sh-should," Jasper added, teeth chattering.

The water running down my neck felt like snowmelt. "Do you think we can make a go of the farm?" I asked finally.

"Yes," he said. "M-maybe."

"We can't go home," I told him. Another thunder crack made us all jump. "Here, now," I said. "Let's sing."

"Wh-what?" Jasper sounded like I'd started speaking in tongues.

"I'm going to teach you a song." I had to think about that, since the little ones already knew all of Mama's tunes. That left me with Ben's favorites. His singing voice was plain but strong enough to carry us through 'most any chore. I settled on "Will Ye Go to Flanders, My Mally-O?" and changed the words a bit:

"Will ye go to Nashville, my Maudie-O?
Will ye go to Nashville, my Mary-O?
There we'll get wine and brandy,
And sack and sugar candy;
Will ye go to Nashville, my Jasper-O?"

On the second round, Jasper joined in. Then Mary. Maude didn't sing, but I thought maybe she hummed along a bit. After I was sure Jasper had it down, I added some harmony. We sang loud as we could, beating back the night.

In the first gray light I looked from the girls, who'd finally curled together and gone to sleep, to Jasper, snoring against one of the wheels. They looked damp and puny as newborn kittens. *Please, God, if you're watching—help Jasper grow up some, because I surely could use more help. Mary tends toward sickly, so please keep her well. As for Maude . . . I'd take it as a most kind turn if you'd let me hear her laugh again. Amen.*

I felt more achy than I did after butchering, or chopping corn, or stripping tobacco—worse than if I'd done all those things at the same time. For hours. On the hottest day of the year. I closed my eyes and tried to pretend I was back in our cabin loft, waiting to hear Mama call us. Waiting to smell flannel cakes. Waiting to hear Papa calling "Sookie sookie sookie!" to the cow, or the ring of his ax at the woodpile. Waiting for Ben to come whistling 'round to help me with chores so we could run off to the hills and dig ramps or gather chestnuts or lie on our backs and stare at the clouds —

"Hannah?" Maude mumbled. She stirred, and a pain zigged through my leg like lightning.

"Jasper, Maude, Mary, face the day." I sighed.

I crawled into the morning. Although the forest still dripped, the rain had passed. But when I looked in the cart, my stomach clenched. Our leather shoes were soaked. Some of the cornmeal was wet. The Bible's leather binding was damp, a few of its page edges already curling like green leaves in a fire. I tried to suck air into my lungs.

"Oh Hannah, the Bible," Jasper whispered.

"I know!" I snapped. "And I am fast taking a powerful dislike to that hound-puppy look of yours!"

He stomped away. I closed my eyes and tried to think. I wanted to take a morning and spread our wet things out to dry. I wanted to air the quilts and let our tin and iron cookware dry before rust set in. But I also felt a powerful pull to keep moving.

I opened my eyes again. "Let's pack up and get going. We'll take a long stop at noon," I promised. Mary nodded. Jasper and Maudie didn't even do that.

The road was a mess of mud that squeezed between our toes, dragged at my hem, crusted on our legs and clothes. We had to wrestle the cart hub-deep through stretches of sucking ooze. Puddles hid rocks and ruts from view, and we stumbled like field hands drunk on too much applejack. As the sun edged higher I almost wished for more rain, because the morning gave birth to a powerful sticky heat.

I let my mind drift to Cumberland Mountain, to the days when we used the McNeills' sorghum press, and in turn gave them half the honey from the bee tree Papa made from a hollow sweet gum log. All of a piece Jasper started flailing and kicking. "Jasper, what?" I cried.

"It's—these—bugs!" he cried, frantically swatting at a cloud of gnats.

"We had gnats on Cumberland Mountain too," I pointed out. But I cut a switch of leafy maple for each of us. "Wave them back and forth while you walk," I said, and we walked on twitching our swatters like cows their tails.

I went back to Cumberland Mountain—a crisp fall day

when woodsmoke mingled with the scent of apple butter simmering in the big kettle in the yard. I stood outside the smokehouse with cold toes, smelling the promise of full bellies in the applewood and bacon squeezing through the cracks between the logs—

"Hannah, I'm tired," Maude whined.

"Let's just go a little farther, Maudie."

"But my feet hurt." Her lower lip pushed out.

"My feet hurt too. But we got to go a bit more."

She toddled on a bit before she just gave in and sat down in the road.

"All right." I sighed, swinging her up to the cart. "You can ride for a spell, and then Mary. One at a time. We need to help Star as much as we can."

Star got a scratch between the ears. I might as well be herding geese to Nashville, for all the help I was getting.

All that day we climbed steep tracks up and down the mountain hollows shaded with oak and poplar and basswood trees. The last bell lilies nodded as we passed. Sometimes we passed little farms, mostly hardscrabble places like ours. A couple of times the road forked. "Which way?" I asked Jasper, and he allowed as how he couldn't quite tell without the map in front of him, and I had to ask directions.

Once I saw a boy with a face speckled as a brook trout, hauling stone from his cornfield on a sled, and I asked if we could water Star at his family's trough. But mostly I tried to hurry by the cabins without stopping. "Don't talk to anyone unless you're sure they're for the Union," I told the little ones.

Jasper scratched his bottom. "Hannah . . . I don't much understand what the Yankee soldiers are fighting and killing and dying for." He clamped his mouth shut.

"I don't understand it myself." I took a deep breath and blew it out again, trying to keep my voice even. "But I guess if Pa thought the Union men were right, they surely are."

"You said you hated Pa," he muttered.

"Sometimes I do," I said. "But if we run across another string of Yankee soldiers, we'll talk to them."

"Pa always said Camerons tend their own."

"I *know.*" I rubbed some sweat from my forehead. "But with him getting himself killed for the Union Army, it seems fair enough to ask them for a bit of help. Maybe they'll share their food with us."

"Or maybe they'll give us a ride to Nashville, seeing that Pa was in their army and all!" He looked at me hopefully.

"Maybe so. Come on, now—this low patch looks bad. Take Star so I can push the cart if need be."

It did need be, for trees penned the road, and in a dip, the mud was almost knee-deep. I helped the twins pick their way through, and then had Jasper tug on Star's halter while I shouldered up to the cart. One wheel sank almost to the hub, and I pushed till I thought my back might snap in two, and still the cart sat stubborn. I gave a mighty heave. My feet slid out from under me. I grabbed the cart and still ended up on my knees in the muck.

"Cursed mud!" I banged my fist against the cart. "We're going to be here all night!"

Poor Star shied like I'd hit her. My shoulders slumped. "Let me catch my breath," I told Jasper, then rested my forehead against the cart and tried not to bawl. I tried to make my mind go empty, but I couldn't help remembering a morning soon after Pa had gone to war when Jasper and I wrestled a plow down a furrow, tired and sticky-hot. Jasper got red with heat, and I finally gave in and sank on the ground. I didn't want to bother Mama but had just about concluded that Jasper and me couldn't get the work done when I heard Ben whistling on the trail. He sent Jasper to the creek and had me lead Star while he took up the plowshares. And he started singing:

"As I was a-wandering in the month of sweet May
I heard a young ploughboy to whistle and to say
And, aye, as he was lamenting these very words he did say,
'There's no life like the ploughboy in the month of sweet
    May.'"

We didn't speak until we had that field done, and Star tended to, and had walked down to the cool dim of the spring-house. "I'm obliged," I'd said, passing him a dipper.

He had shrugged. "We work pretty well together, seems to me." Those dark eyes had held my gaze over the tin dipper, even while he gulped cold water. I could still see him there, his linen shirt stained with sweat, the air smelling like moss and the spring burbling—

"Hannah?" Jasper called. "You been taken sick back there?"

"No." I hauled myself up, found the best footholds I could,

and leaned into the cart. "Up, Star! Up now!" And with a mighty groan and heave the cart wrenched forward again.

As we headed on we passed an old red oak tree, downed by a storm. It was mostly dead, all brown leaves and such, except for one tiny bit growing proud and green from the stump, straight toward the sun. "Ben," I whispered, "did you ever see such?" And in my mind he allowed that no, he'd never seen such, and that maybe we should study on that oak tree and try to figure it all out.

Then Ben's voice faded. Purely disappeared.

I took one last look at that green branch before passing by. I had to be like that.

Chapter 4

We made our way out of the hills toward bigger roads. We walked south in the shadow of Stone Mountain, then turned west and followed the Emery Road. Coming out in the open, walking a valley road, made me feel like a baby rabbit out where every vulture might see.

Jasper gawked at the bigger farms we passed, with fields flat as could be. Most had weeds in the corn, this being wartime and all. But they were still something to behold. "I wouldn't mind having me a place like that someday," he said, more than once. I didn't answer.

At night we lay beneath the open sky. "I heard once that sailors steer by the stars," he told me. "They can fix their ships toward China, just by the stars. China! Now, wouldn't that be something to see?"

"Go to sleep," I said.

When I asked directions one morning from some folks on a store porch, an old man with no teeth and a cheek full of tobacco mumbled something about walking the valley toward Jacksboro.

We headed in the direction of his pointed finger. "I wonder what's down the other way," Jasper said, craning his neck back toward the fork we hadn't taken.

"Not Aunt Ellen!" I reminded him. "Come along!"

One day when we stopped for a nooning amidst a patch of joe-pye weed, we heard the rumble and rattle of a heavy wagon coming toward us. Soon a man drove a big wagon around the bend, pulled by a pair of oxen. A woman and four or five kids walked alongside, every one of them wearing shoes. A tall bureau with shiny metal fixings stuck up in the middle of barrels and bulging carpetbags. A withered-apple old woman sat hunched in a rocking chair, swaying with every lurch of the wagon. She wore a shiny black bonnet trimmed with lace.

"You burned out too?" the man called.

"You might say so," I said carefully.

The man spat over the wagon seat. "*Bushwhackers.* We're headed to Knoxville. You?"

"Nashville. We got kin," I added quickly.

"Best head to Knoxville. Nashville's too far. You'll never make it to Nashville." Then the wagon rattled on past, and the man turned back to the trail. The woman and children never stopped, never even glanced our way.

The man's voice echoed in my head for the rest of the afternoon: *You'll never make it to Nashville.* Oh yes, we will, I thought. The words beat time with my own stubborn footsteps. *We will. We will. We will.*

That worked for me, and I let the girls each ride another spell in the cart, but Jasper plodded with his head hung down like a whipped hound's. "Jasper!" I called. "What do you know about China?"

"Nothing," he muttered.

I tried to let him be then, but finally got tired of slowing up to wait for him. "Pick up your feet! You're moving like molasses flowing uphill."

He made a face. "Let's stop for the night."

"It's too early. We've got to put more miles behind us."

"I'm worn to a nub," he whined.

I let go of Star's halter and planted my hands on my hips. "Well, I'm worn to a nub too! I've walked as far as you have! And I have to take charge of you three while I'm at it!"

Jasper plunked down in the road, glaring. "Nobody asked you to take charge! We don't have to listen to what you say. I'd rather sit here till first freeze than listen to you. I'd rather go back to the neighbors than listen to you—"

"*Jasper!*" I took root in the road. Mary went still as stone in the cart. "Hush up your fighting," Maude begged, laying her cheek against Dolly.

I didn't notice the Negro woman until she was almost in spitting range.

"Fine day," she called. She was a scrawny thing, fence-rail-thin, traveling with a blanket roll slung over her shoulder and a basket in one hand. The skirt of her blue cotton dress was as crusted with mud as mine. The calico scarf knotted over her hair was dusty. She wore a man's ragged sack coat over her dress. Maybe that was easier than carrying it, even in the sticky heat.

She stopped by the cart, looking from me to the little ones. "I said, fine day." Her voice was soft.

"Um . . . yes, ma'am," I stammered. I'd never actually spoken to a colored person before. I'd only seen a few in all my born days, mostly hanging at the back during big outdoor preachings and such.

The woman shook her head. "You poor children look like you've walked a hard mile. Is that so?" She looked at me with eyes that somehow seemed older than the rest of her. Weary eyes. But kindly too. They 'minded me a bit—just a bit—of Mama's eyes, after Pa went off to war.

"Yes, ma'am." I wondered if she was a slave or free. None of the scratch-dirt farm families on Cumberland Mountain, or even down to Walnut Cove, owned any slaves. I'd heard tell that a couple of free black families lived a few miles east of our place, toward the North Carolina line, but they kept to their own. I didn't know if there was a way to tell free black from slave just by looking.

She rummaged in her basket. "Seems like I might have a bite or two of gingerbread left. Here." She found a chunk of dark gingerbread, which she carefully broke into four pieces. "You want a bite, child?" She offered the first piece to Mary.

"Thank you kindly," Mary said.

Maude looked to me for approval and I nodded, suddenly remembering hearing some of the men back home saying that there wouldn't be any more slaves because President Lincoln, up north, had signed a paper making them free. "Won't mean a dang thing until the Yankees show up to make it so," Preacher had said, sending a stream of tobacco juice square at a gatepost. I hadn't thought of that, the day the Yankees marched past our place.

The woman gave Maude and Jasper their pieces of gingerbread, then held one out to me. Her hand had the hard, big-knuckled look of someone who knew well the feel of a grub hoe or ax handle. The palm of her hand wasn't black like the rest of her. It was more like the color of new peaches or a swallow's belly, except in the cracks and crannies, where it was darker again.

That gingerbread was spicy and rich and best of all, not made of cornmeal. I chewed slow as I could and still it was gone in a shake. The others had gobbled theirs like hungry hogs.

"Well, I got a long road ahead. Looks like you do too." The woman tucked the cloth cover back over her basket and turned away.

"Wait!" I called. "Here—ma'am . . . Oh Mary, move over." I poked into one of our food sacks and came up with some dried apple rings, and handed them over.

A slow smile split the woman's face, almost—but not quite—reaching those tired eyes. She ate those rings one at a time. Then she put her hand on my shoulder for a moment. It felt warm, right through my dress. "Don't you got a mama to tend you?"

I shook my head. "But we've got kin." I hesitated, my mind bubbling like a forgotten stewpot. Somehow I couldn't bring my tongue to ask what I most wanted to know. "Where you headed?" I finally managed.

"Well, I don't rightly know." She tipped her head to one side, considering, then nodded. "But I do know I'm free to go there. Yes ma'am, I'm free to wander."

Jasper licked his fingers one more time. "Don't you have kin somewhere?"

"Somewhere. Yes, somewhere." She rubbed at a stain on her dress. It looked like pokeberries. "My husband, he got sold off. My children too. But I'm free now. We're all free. Free to wander."

With that she hooked her basket back over her arm and set off slowly down the road. In a moment she rounded a bend and disappeared.

Jasper shoved to his feet. "Hannah . . . was that woman a slave?"

"Used to be one, I guess."

"I heard Preacher and Mr. Duncan talking once, a while ago, and they said the Yankees were turning this war into a war to free the slaves. Is that right?"

"Well, I heard so too." I was trying to recollect why white people thought they were better than colored people. I couldn't remember ever hearing a reason. I'd never had call to think on it one way or another, but now that I *was* thinking on it, I didn't see a lick of sense to the whole notion.

I didn't have all day to stand there and ponder. I reached for Mary and swung her to the ground. "You've had a good rest. You can walk a bit again. Jasper, lead Star for a spell, will you?"

Jasper didn't move. "Hannah . . . did Papa go off to help free the slaves?"

I sighed. "The war wasn't about the slaves, back when it all got started. You didn't hear the Rebel folks we knew going about hollering for slavery, did you?" I wished Papa *had* gone off to fight to free slaves. That was a reason with some meat to it.

I tugged Star's halter, and we all got started again. Jasper kept close. "How do you figure Ben felt about the war taking a turn to free the slaves, his family being Rebel and all?"

"Jasper, I wish you would stop chattering about Ben McNeill!"

He frowned. "Cripes, Hannah, I just—"

"Oh, I know." After a moment I allowed, "I can't imagine Ben—or his pa—fighting to save rich folks the right to own slaves."

Mary tugged my dress. "Hannah, that gingerbread was good."

"Yes, it was." I took her hand. "And that might have been her last bite of food." I thought about the white family we'd seen earlier that day, with a full wagon and nothing for us but deadly warnings. I wished I'd asked that Negro woman her name.

We kept heading west.

When we reached the Emery River I had to pay an oxlike man half of our precious coins to ferry us across on a raft. I hadn't known about that. There was nothing to do but take the ride, and keep walking.

Our feet toughed up till I was sure I could crack a chestnut burr beneath my bare heel as easy as with my shoe. Our legs got stronger and that helped some too. In the mornings we sang while we tramped along, with Mary and even Maudie piping in. We had a particular favorite that Papa used to sing:

> *"The Camerons be comin', Oho! Oho!*
> *We're braw and we're bonnie, you know, you know!*
> *The Camerons be comin', we'll send the foe runnin',*
> *The Camerons be comin', Oho! Oho!"*

"What's *braw*?" Jasper asked.

"It means 'brave,' I think," I said, and he smiled.

One afternoon we passed a little frame church, with buggies and wagons parked outside and a row of skinny horses hitched at the rail. When I heard singing drift through the open windows, I stopped in my tracks. "Let's just rest here a minute," I whispered to the others.

"Really?" Maude asked, but all three had already plopped down in the shade of a handy oak tree.

"It won't do us a lick of harm to hear a psalm or two sung." I closed my eyes, letting the music flow inside like a river, sweet and cool. It even splashed into the Ben-hole beneath my ribs.

Once our two families had gone to a camp meeting in Walnut Cove. The visiting preacher had brought a choir, and they sounded like angels themselves come down to earth. I picked out four different parts in their harmony—and here I'd thought two was the grace of God itself! A few days later, when Ben and I were shelling peas for his mother, I'd dared, "I have this notion . . . I dream about maybe one day singing in a choir. Like at that camp meeting."

Ben had scowled. "I dream of Cumberland Mountain."

"Hannah, shouldn't we get going?" Jasper asked.

"In a bit." I closed my eyes and tried to disappear back into the singing.

Someone put a small finger on my arm. "Hannah, we have to walk some more," Mary said.

I walked mighty slow until the last notes faded away behind us.

Best as I could, I kept track of our progress as the days passed. Sometimes I questioned someone we met—"How far are we from Nashville?"—comparing the distance with our food supply. It had taken almost three weeks to hit the halfway mark, instead of the ten days I'd figured. Fear nibbled, but I shoved it back. Strawberry season was long past, but blackberries were ripe. Maybe Jasper could gig a frog or two. We'd get by.

I was frying breakfast corn cakes as I did my figuring, and made them a bit smaller than usual. But I decided to tell the others that we'd made it halfway. It was something to celebrate. "Breakfast is about ready," I called, using a fork to turn the corn cakes. "And I want to tell you something—"

"Hannah, look!" Maude whispered.

I followed her wide-eyed stare. A man in a blue uniform was limping toward us. A musket rested against his shoulder. "Hallo!" he called.

Jasper jerked around from packing the cart. Maude ducked behind a tree, and Mary followed her. I stood up.

"Didn't mean to startle you none," the soldier said. He was

of middling age, with a bushy brown beard. "The name's Jack. I smelled your smoke. Mind if I share your fire?" Still favoring one foot, he eased down.

"Sure, sit a spell," I offered. Jack formed some of his words queer, but that blue uniform made me feel almost like Pa had come to join us. He was the first Yankee we'd seen since the day Mama died. . . . I gulped some air to get steady. "Hannah," I said in answer. "That's my brother, Jasper, and my sisters, Maudie and Mary." Maude was still hiding, but Mary peeked around her tree trunk.

"They remind me of my own little ones back home." Jack heaved a big sigh. "I'm from Vermont."

I didn't know where Vermont was. "I bet you miss your family."

"Oh, sure. But mostly I just want to rest my feet for a piece before moving on." Jack's army brogans were cracked and tattered. He'd bound twine around his left foot to hold the upper and sole together, but his toes peeked out. He scrabbled in a little leather sack slung over one shoulder. "Look what I got!" He pulled out a chunk of brown bread and several small sweet potatoes. "Would you share a meal with me?"

"Why . . . that's right kind of you!" Most of the travelers we saw had ghosts in their eyes and kept to themselves. We hadn't seen nice since that slave woman shared her gingerbread. I flipped my last corn cake from the skillet onto a plate. "We're glad to share our dodgers too." That gave Jack the short end of the deal, but if he didn't mind, I wasn't going to complain.

Mary tugged on Maude's hand, and they crept closer. Jasper squatted beside the fire, watching Jack slice the sweet potatoes into the hot skillet. They popped and sizzled in promise. "Our pa was in the Union Army too," Jasper said.

"Was he? Well, well." Jack poked at his flapping shoe, frowning. "And where is your pa now?"

"Dead," Jasper said. "Mama too. We're going to our aunt Ellen in Nashville."

"Well, now, that's a tragedy." Jack shook his head. "I'd like to wring the necks of whoever had the whole idea for this war."

"Where's the rest of the army?" I asked. "We saw a line of Yankee troops go past our place a few weeks back. A whole passel of 'em."

"Closest camp is thirty miles or so west of here, near as I can tell. I'm headed that way." Jack stirred the potatoes with a fork.

My mouth began to water. "How come you're off on your own?"

Jack rubbed his chin. "Well, I was on picket duty—keeping watch, you might say—and I got bit by a snake. A copperhead, somebody said." He pulled up one trouser leg, and I saw two angry crusted-over slashes just above the ankle, where somebody had cut the bite open to suck the poison out. "Didn't even see the thing till I stepped on it."

Jasper shook his head. "That's hard luck."

"We don't have copperheads in Vermont. Here." Jack pulled the skillet from the fire and scraped most of the potatoes onto our waiting plates. He dug into what was left, straight from the frypan. "It's a god-awful climate you folks got down here," he mumbled around a mouthful. "All sorts of critters waiting to do a body harm."

"Tennessee is a pretty fair place, once you come to know it," I said, taking a pause between bites. "And the serpents, they mostly try to warn you off. They're fair enough, Ben—well, a friend—used to say. Rattlers shake their tails. Copperheads are quiet, but they give off a garden smell, almost like cucumbers, before they bite. I've never seen a cottonmouth moccasin, but folks say they open their mouths wide before they strike, and their mouths are white inside, and you see that and know. . . ."

My voice slid away. Jack was staring at me like I'd gone addled. I hadn't realized just how hungry I was for *talk*. My face grew warm, and I fixed on finishing my sweet potatoes. They did taste fine.

"You know those varmints pretty good," Jack said after a bit. "Me, I'm like a fish out of water in these woods."

I couldn't tell if he was poking fun my way. "Lived here all my life," I mumbled.

"Well, anyhow . . . I took sick after that bite, and got left behind. A farmwife took me in, but she was nervy about it."

I nodded. With good reason! One Yankee, left behind in Confederate country . . . just the thing to bring down the bushwhackers. Suddenly I felt a whisper of nervy myself. Suppose some Confederates happened down the road while Jack was with us?

Hannah Cameron, you should be ashamed! Are you so craven as to turn away a soldier from your own pa's army? One who's been snakebit and left behind but still shared his breakfast? Are you really such a coward?

"I hit out soon as I could walk again," Jack was saying, "aiming to catch up with the army. But it's slow going. My leg's still sore."

"It surely is slow going," Jasper agreed. "Even without running into a copperhead." He'd finished his potatoes and a goodly chunk of bread, and only now reached for one of the corn cakes.

Jack finished eating, set the frypan aside, and shoved to his feet. "Speaking of, I should be moving on."

"I guess so," I said quickly, feeling relieved. I still had dishes to do. I'd let Jack get a good head start before we set out too.

But Jack didn't move. He paused, wiping his hands on his pants, looking around the clearing. He nodded toward Star. "You got yourself a fine-looking mule there."

"She's old. But she does what she needs to do." Just *go*, I thought. Go before some Confederate comes by.

But Jack didn't go. Instead he stood like a fence post, staring at Star. He opened his mouth. Shut it again. Chewed his lip. That nervy feeling coiled in my belly and shook its tail in warning. Two wrens argued overhead. A breeze whispered among the hemlocks overhead.

Then Jack's foot crunched on dead leaves. He didn't head toward the road. He headed toward Star.

ᴄᴧᴧ Chapter 5 ᴧᴧᴧ

I jumped up. "What are you doing?"

"I'll trade you for her. All the food I got. And my money too." Jack pulled off his leather pouch and shoved it at me.

I shoved it right back. "No!"

"Listen to me!" He grabbed my arm. "I'm not trying to do you a harsh turn. But I need that mule more than you do—"

"We need her to get to Nashville!"

"You can get by without her! You're not the one with nothing to wear but this cursed Union uniform! And you know this country. You even know how to talk to snakes! You can get by a whole lot better out here than me." He sounded like a boy pleading for the first taste at sugaring time.

I poured all the gravel I had into one word: *"No!"*

Jack hung his head. The wrens still chittered overhead. The little ones had frozen. And for a moment I thought I'd won.

Then Jack tossed his leather bag. It landed at my feet. "There's a few more sweet potatoes in here, and a sack of sugar. And some coins."

He had his hand on Star's halter before I found my tongue again. "You can't take Star!"

"I figure I can." He leaned his gun against the cart and began picking at the knot in Star's picket line. "I'm sorry to do you young'uns a bad turn. But I need this mule."

My breath came in little heaves. *The gun*, I thought. If I can get to the gun—

Suddenly Jasper flew across the clearing like a bat from the barn. "NO!" he bellowed, and slammed into Jack.

"Girls, run!" I yelled. They bolted into the trees.

Jasper whaled away, all pounding fists and kicking feet. The big soldier stumbled, then found his balance and swung an arm with the practiced ease of a grain cradler. Jasper tumbled aside.

I caught my brother in my arms. When I looked back, Jack had his musket leveled toward us. "Don't make me do something worse." He had the brass to sound miserable.

Jasper struggled, and I hugged him tighter. "Hannah, we can't lose Star!" he whimpered.

"It's not worth getting killed," I hissed. "It's not."

And I tried to believe it as Jack freed Star from her picket line, fashioned the rope into a makeshift bridle, and swung to her back. Star shied a bit, not used to him, but he tugged on the rope. "Come on, mule," he said, drumming his heels against her bony flanks. With a snort she lunged forward. Jack bounced like a sack of potatoes but managed to hang on as they trotted onto the road. In a moment they disappeared around a bend.

Jasper wrenched free. "Hannah, he's got Star!" he sobbed. "What are we going to do?"

"I don't know!" I found myself back on the ground, staring at the empty road. A Union soldier couldn't have just stolen Star. I waited to see them come back, Jack laughing about his joke.

"He took Star!" Maude wept.

"I know." The road was still empty.

"But Star belongs to us!" Mary quavered.

"Hannah," Jasper began again, "what are we going to do?"

"Why do I always have to be the one to figure things out? Just hush your mouth, all of you."

I couldn't bear watching the road's stillness anymore. I crawled toward the fire, snapped off the tip of a spruce branch, and scoured that skillet like it was Jack's hide. The others watched me like scared rabbits. "I'm going to make us some tea," I finally said, sighing. "Jasper, fetch some kindling, will you? And just—just don't say anything for a bit."

I built up the fire, filled the skillet, and propped it on the rocks I'd positioned the night before. When the water was hot I added the mint leaves, watching them slowly stain the water as they steeped. I thought about adding some of Jack's sugar— Lordy be, sugar!—but the notion turned my stomach. I poured myself a cup of tea. One for Jasper. One for Mary. One for Maude.

Jasper pitched a twig into the fire. "He was a *Union* man."

"I know," I said slowly. How could a Union soldier, some- one from my own pa's army, do such a thing? Then I remem- bered that whoever had burned out Ben McNeill and his family had been Unionist too, like Jack. Like us.

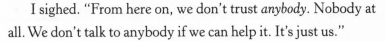

I sighed. "From here on, we don't trust *anybody*. Nobody at all. We don't talk to anybody if we can help it. It's just us."

"Just us," Jasper agreed bitterly. He threw a stone at a tree—hard. Finally he asked again, very quietly, "Hannah, what are we going to do?"

I blew out a long breath. "The cart's too heavy for us to pull ourselves. We'll have to leave it. Girls, you're . . . you're going to have to walk. Jasper, you and I will have to divvy up what we can carry."

Jasper chewed his lip like an old man. "On to Nashville? Or back home?"

"On to Nashville. We're about halfway." I felt a sudden urge to laugh—to think I'd been saving that news to cheer them on! I didn't want my brain to start figuring how long it would take to walk to Nashville without the cart, and how much food we could carry.

"You figure we can make it?"

"We've got to," I said, flat as a flannel cake. "We can walk to Nashville, or we can sit here and starve."

Walk to Nashville. Just saying those words out loud, spooky as they were, shored up my backbone. I had a plan.

"Hannah," Jasper said slowly. "I think we should go back."

I stared at him like a great horned owl. "What do you mean?"

"Just what I said."

"But—why go back? Go back just to get split up among the Duncans and the O'Briens and the Peabodys? Is that what you want?"

Jasper sat on the far side of the fire with his arms folded firm across his chest. "It's not what I want. But it's better than this."

"It—it *is* better than this," I allowed. "But if we keep going, we'll end up at a place with kin. We've got to stay together, Jasper."

"Why do you get to make all the decisions, and order us around?"

"Someone's got to!"

Jasper fixed me with a glare. "You're not my ma!"

"But I'm the oldest—"

"And I'm the boy! And when Pa left, he told me I had to be the man of the family while he was gone."

"Well, you sure haven't acted like the man of the family! You've acted like a wee boy. I'd be in Nashville by now if I didn't have to mollycoddle you three every step of the way—"

"*Mollycoddle!*" Jasper's eyes squeezed down to slits. "If it's such a chore to mollycoddle us, Hannah Cameron, then you can quit right now. We'll just head back home without you."

I grabbed his arm. "You listen to me, Jasper," I hissed, ready to shake all the ornery nonsense out of him. But that arm felt fragile in my hand, like a bird bone. I bit my tongue, looking him up and down. Maybe he wanted to be the man of the family. Truth was, he was just a skinny, tired boy missing his folks.

I took a deep breath. "Jasper, I'm sorry. Truly. And to you too, girls." I tossed a sorry look toward the two girls, sitting shoulder to shoulder. "I didn't mean to holler." I rubbed my forehead. "I know you're upset about losing Star. I know you want to go back home. You know what? I do too, more than anything. But Mama wanted us to stay together, and this is the only way."

"I'd feel more kindly about staying together if you hadn't turned so mean," Jasper muttered, digging a hole in the dirt with his big toe.

"Mean? Why—I—I . . ." I sputtered out like a kettle boiled dry. Had I been so hard on him?

My folks were spare with talk, but they'd had ways of letting us know when we'd done them proud. "You've hickory in you, Hannah," Papa would say, nodding, if I'd weaned a cross calf or worn myself out building a straw stack that would shed rain. He meant I was strong as hickory, someone he could lean on for help. And Mama would reward a careful seam or savory stew with one of her quiet smiles.

I sighed. "Jasper, I'm proud of you. I should have said before that you done real good back there, with that Union soldier. I didn't want you to get killed. But I'm proud that you tried to save Star. You've got hickory in you."

"Well . . . really?"

"Really." I turned to the girls. "I'm proud of you both too. I don't want to be mean. I'm just trying to do what Mama wanted. All right?"

"All right," Mary echoed, and I saw Maude's lips move too. I looked at Jasper. He nodded.

"I can get us to Nashville," I promised. "But I'm leaning on you." And another memory almost laid me low: Pa, right before he left, saying the same thing to me. I hadn't answered. Hadn't known how much it would have meant to him.

But Jasper, bless him, did better. "I'll try harder, Hannah," he promised quietly and straightened his thin shoulders in a way that made me want to bawl like a lost calf.

Just then we heard the creak and rumble of wooden wheels jolting over the rough road. When a cart jostled clear of the trees, Jasper jumped to his feet. Maude and Mary ran. I wiped my eyes again and squinted back at the road, bewildered.

It was the McNeills.

Ben led their mule, hitched to their own two-wheeled cart. His sister, Sary, walked beside with a big basket on one hip. Mrs. McNeill sat in the cart, hunched over like she wasn't well.

Ben's feet quit moving. He stared. I stared back, my body tight, half-waiting for him to start throwing rocks again. If he had, I would have pitched into him the way Jasper had pitched into Jack. Half of me ached for the chance.

The other half of me ached for Ben to come over. I wanted him to say "What the jigger happened here?" and listen while I told him about Star, and talk the whole mess through with me.

But after a long moment he turned his head. Just turned back to the road like we were strangers. "Get up!" he said to the mule, and the cart lurched forward. Sary followed. Mrs. McNeill hadn't even lifted her head.

We watched until they disappeared, and the creak and rumble faded into silence. "I guess they're going to Nashville too," Jasper said finally.

"I guess so." I stared at the empty road. Jack hadn't changed his mind, but maybe Ben would. Maybe he'd turn around, come back to help us.

A squirrel darted across the road. Nothing else moved.

I turned back to our cart. "Come on," I said, and heard the iron in my voice. "We got to sort out our things. Girls! Come out now. It's safe."

I took Jack's coins but couldn't stomach taking anything else of his. Jasper and I fashioned bundles from two of the quilts and filled them with makeshift sacks of cornmeal. I felt like I had a stone in my chest as I tried to decide how much we could carry. I didn't give the girls anything to carry but their shoes slung around their necks, and Maude brought the doll. I gave Jasper what I thought he could manage. He hefted it, then silently added a few more handfuls of cornmeal from our half-barrel before tying up the quilt into an awkward bundle. Then he slung it over his shoulder. "We best get moving, don't you think?"

"Yes," I said, but I turned back to the cart one last time. Jasper had the family tintypes in his pocket. Mama's ring was on the string around my neck. The wool plaid was rolled into my bundle.

But we couldn't take the Bible.

I touched the cover, a little fuzzy with mold from the soaking it had gotten. I flipped through pages where Mama and Pa had looked for strength and comfort. I stopped when I reached the section where generations of Camerons had written of births and marriages and deaths. Three pages had writing, the ink already faded. Holding my breath, I pinched those pages and slowly tore them free. The ripping sound rang like blasphemy.

"Hannah!" Jasper gasped.

I folded the pages, then slipped them into my apron pocket.

"I can't carry the Bible," I managed. My fingers strayed to the ring with the green stone, hidden on the string beneath my dress. I squeezed it tight. Then I turned my back on the cart.

We walked for maybe an hour before clouds shoved over the sun. I heard thunder rumbling down the valley for a while before the morning turned dark as dusk. We couldn't find shelter by the time the storm reached us. In the end we crouched beneath an elm tree while the rain slashed down and lightning cracked across the sky. Maybe God sent the storm to punish me for ripping pages out of the Holy Book.

We waited out the worst of it under that tree before setting out again, drenched to the marrow and shivering cold. When I pinched up the courage to peek down into my apron pocket, I saw three folded pages stuck together, the ink from long-dead Camerons now run and smeared and ruined. I waited till the others weren't looking, then scraped every shred of damp paper from my pocket and threw them beside the road.

We walked and walked and walked, until our feet were on fire and our legs felt like wood. The days ran together, an endless string of days spent on the road while cicadas buzzed in the woods and the sun crept slowly across the sky, and forever nights spent trying to sleep in thickets or hidden in fencerows.

We trudged along hungry, like as not. The garden sass was long gone. The dried fruit went next, then the rice. Mostly we lived on cornmeal mush. I'd left our little crock of lard in the cart when we lost Star, so I couldn't even fry corn cakes. We managed to find a few blackberries, and sometimes some watercress. I gave our last pennies to a woman at an inn for a bowl of pork and hominy that disappeared all too quick.

Once we passed a sorry-looking farm, a place with trees still poking up through the corn and sorghum. A red-faced woman with a neck like a gander was using an ax to girdle an oak near the fence while we passed, hacking off the bark in a clean circle so the tree would die. Time was, that was man's work.

"Excuse me, ma'am," I called, "which fork to Nashville?"

She let the ax dangle and pointed, breathing hard. I nodded and turned to go, but she found breath to yell, "It's almost seventy miles to Nashville! You young'uns ain't going to make it to Nashville."

I turned my back on her. "The Camerons are coming, Oho! Oho!" I began to sing, and kept walking.

We saw more and more people like us on the road—homeless, hungry, all trying to get somewhere else. Some were Negroes. Most were white. They came on foot and in carts, in threadbare homespun and faded silk. Some had wagons loaded crazily with picture frames and oak furniture and heirloom china. More carried nothing save a blanket roll and a hungry look in their eyes.

As the next week passed—our fourth on the road—my dress began to hang on me like I was a scarecrow. Jasper's suspenders were all that stood between him and a mighty embarrassment. Mary developed a wheezy, thin cough that seemed to rattle her bones. And Maude's face seemed all eyes . . . big round eyes that I saw even when I shut my own. At night she slept clutching Dolly, and her tin cup and spoon too. "They're mine!" she cried, the first time I tried to ease them from her hand, so I let her be.

I did try to find more food. "Camerons tend their own, aye?" Papa said sternly in memory, every time I asked some stranger for help. I was surely glad Ben McNeill was somewhere ahead of us now, and couldn't see me sunk so low. But I did it for the little ones, always offering to trade chores for a meal when we came upon a middling-size farm by the road and folks working outside. The first time I did it, a woman in a faded red sunbonnet gave me an apron full of green beans in exchange for us chopping enough wood to fill her woodbox. That afternoon a woman gave us half a cabbage and wouldn't even take a chore done in trade.

The next day I stopped at another farm, one where there were still chickens to scratch in the dirt, and an ox to pull a plow. It was a frame house, not log, and I could see a man pitching hay around a rick pole beyond the barn, so I figured things might not be too bad. But when I approached a woman pegging out laundry, she turned on me like I was a devil. "Off with you!" she cried, before I'd more than opened my mouth. "I can't have every one of you coming round! Move on!" She flapped her apron like we were stray dogs.

My hands fisted as we walked back to the road. "Mean old thing," Jasper muttered. He plopped down in the dust.

"Yes she was," I agreed. "Hateful. I hate her!"

Jasper threw a rock across the road. "Maybe we should just wait until night and go back and dig something out of the garden."

I shook my head. "*No.* Camerons know the difference between right and wrong."

Jasper stared at the ground for a moment, then shoved to his feet. "Let's get moving," he said gruffly.

By late afternoon we were walking in single file. I had taken to bringing up the rear so I could keep an eye on the other three. I watched Mary trudge in front of me, head drooping. Maude's arm slowly dropped until Dolly dragged in the dust. Then the doll slipped from her fingers altogether. Maude didn't seem to notice.

I stopped and stared at Dolly. Mama had made her from scraps of our own clothes, in late evenings when her other chores were done. I picked the doll up and shook it over my head toward the sky. "Pa, look at this!" I hissed.

Jasper and the girls were still plodding along. I sucked in a deep breath and blew it out slow. After swiping some dust from the doll, I tucked it inside my own blanket roll, thinking to surprise Maude with it later. Then I walked after them.

One evening I scraped the last of our cornmeal into our little skillet for evening mush.

"Hannah, do we have any more cornmeal?" Maude asked.

"Nary a bit." I tried to sound like my stomach wasn't twisted into a sick knot of worry. Then I saw the look in Jasper's eyes. *Don't say it,* I willed him. Don't give it words and make it real.

When we settled down that night, I took extra time with the girls' hair. Mary sat still but hardly seemed to notice. Maude asked for a song but didn't sigh and snuggle close. "A-combing down her yellow hair," I sang, gently picking a bit of leaf from Maude's tangled hair. "And her skin was like a lily so fair; her cheeks were like two roses and her eyes were like a star. . . ." I had to steady my voice. "And her voice was like a nightingale clear."

Worry chased its tail in my head long after pure dark stretched over us. Near as I could tell, we were still about fifty miles from Nashville. We were also nearing the Caney Fork River, and I had no money left for the ferry.

We'll have to find our own food, I thought. In the morning, when I wasn't so tired, I'd look for greens. Lamb's-quarter should be ready. I remembered picking a mess of 'em for Mrs. McNeill once, with Ben, and she cooked the shredded leaves with chopped onion and bacon, some cider vinegar, and salt and pepper. . . .

I jerked straight up like I'd been poked. The sun was bright. How had I slept past first light? I could hardly remember where I was, or why. I rubbed my eyes and looked around. Maude and Mary were still asleep—

But Jasper was gone. His blanket roll was gone too.

That popped me to my feet. "Jasper?" I called. "Jasper!" No answer.

Mary jerked awake, rubbing her eyes. "What's wrong? Where'd Jasper go?"

"I don't know." I looked around again, willing him to appear from the trees. When he didn't I bellowed his name again: "JAS-PER!"

Still no answer.

I twisted my fingers together, trying to think. We never got out of hollering distance. My heart began pounding like a black-smith.

"Come on." I quick slung the blanket roll over my shoulder, grabbed the girls' hands, and dragged them out to the road. Which way? Where would he have gone? Fear joined the hunger gnawing at my belly.

"Where did he go?" Maude whimpered.

"I don't know. But we're going to find him." I chose to head west. On toward Nashville.

A refugee family traveling west by oxcart passed, and the woman leading the team said they hadn't seen a lone boy. A fat man on a skinny horse heading east passed too, and he hadn't seen Jasper either. Should we have stayed put?

"Ow!" Maude wrenched her hand from my squeeze. Tears rimmed those big eyes.

"I'm sorry. . . ." I stood stump still, trying to breathe. What should we do? Go forward? Go back?

Then, suddenly, my head jerked toward Nashville. Mary stuck her nose in the air like a coon dog, then Maude. They'd caught it too . . . the faint smells of coffee and frying bacon.

We lit out walking again. In a moment I saw flashes of movement through the brush, heard a mule bray, smelled hickory smoke. We rounded a bend in the road and stopped.

A heavy farm wagon with a tall canvas covering stood parked in a grassy clearing. A rifle leaned against it. Four mules were staked nearby. A man stood beside a small cookfire. His back was to us, and I saw a farmer's shirt, vest, worn trousers, high boots.

And my brother was crouched in front of him. My fear flicked to anger. "*Drat* that boy!" I muttered. "He ran off to find breakfast without giving us a thought—"

Then I realized that Jasper was huddled with his arms crossed in front of his chest. The man grabbed his arm and gave it a shake. I couldn't hear what he was saying, but the low mutter was angry.

"Girls, hide right here," I whispered, and they slid behind trees. I slipped across the clearing and grabbed the man's rifle from its resting place. The gun was heavier than I was used to. But I knew how to cock the hammer back, swing it to my shoulder, and aim.

"Let him go," I hollered.

That man whipped around. Now—*now*—I could see the pistol hanging by his hip. He was young, not much older than

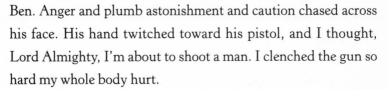

Ben. Anger and plumb astonishment and caution chased across his face. His hand twitched toward his pistol, and I thought, Lord Almighty, I'm about to shoot a man. I clenched the gun so hard my whole body hurt.

Then the man held both hands out from his sides. "Look, now," he tried, "I don't know what you're so riled up about there—"

"Jasper, get up. Come over by me." He obeyed, head hung low. "That's my brother," I told the man. "I don't much like finding him being poorly used." My arms wanted to shake.

"Poorly used!" Rage flared back to life in the man's eyes. "I caught that boy stealing a basket of eggs! Right out of my wagon! He's lucky I didn't tan his hide!"

"*Jasper!*" I turned on him, and the man bolted forward and snatched the rifle from my hands.

"And then some switch of a girl comes along and turns my own gun on me," he blazed. "Why, I oughta—I oughta just . . . tarnation!" He stomped back toward the fire. Kicked a log. Stomped back, with his free hand clenched in a fist.

What would the twins do if he beat me and Jasper? Or shot us stone dead? I put my arms around Jasper and waited for the blow.

Instead the man put the rifle down and grabbed both of us by an arm. "Now you listen to me, and listen good," he growled. "I don't know what you're doing out here on your own. But if there's one thing I can't abide, it's a thief." He gave us each a shake. "You want something from somebody, you ask for it. Hear?"

"I hear," Jasper mumbled. The man's glare bored into me,

which wasn't quite fair, since I wasn't the one caught stealing. But it didn't seem wise to argue. "I hear."

"And you, sneaking up and pointing a rifle—you could have killed somebody. Could have killed *him*." He jerked his head toward Jasper. "Or could have got shot yourself. I've never seen such a fool thing."

He let go of us. I rubbed my arm, sure it would be purple and green by nightfall. "We're sorry," I managed, giving Jasper a glare of my own.

"Yeah. Sorry." Jasper was talking to the ground.

I grabbed his wrist. "We'll be going now—"

"Oh no you won't!" The man scowled at Jasper again, planting his hands on his hips. "Not until you tell me why you were trying to steal in the first place."

Jasper scuffed a toe in the dirt, growing a scowl of his own. "I'm hungry," he mumbled.

"What?"

"I said I'm hungry!" he blazed. "You got plenty!" He turned to me. "He's got a whole wagon plumb full, Hannah, you should see—"

"That doesn't give you the right to steal!" I snapped, although the thought of a basket of eggs made my mouth juice up with hope.

I lifted my chin a notch. "Look, mister, I'm real sorry he tried to steal from you," I told the man. "He was raised better. I can make it right by you, if you've got some chores that need doing."

The man folded his arms across his chest. "Why didn't you just ask me for something?" he asked Jasper.

Jasper hitched his shoulders up and down. "I'm tired of asking. Tired of begging. I just wanted to get a meal for my sisters."

The man looked around. "There's more of you?"

Jasper and I exchanged a glance, uneasy. Was it safe to say? "Two," I finally allowed.

"Well, go get them." I hesitated, and he shook his head. "Do you want breakfast or not?"

Breakfast. Sweet, sweet breakfast. "We don't need charity," I made myself say. "We can chop firewood, or—"

"Lord help us!" The man raised his hands to the heavens, then fixed us with a hard look. "Lesson one: if you need something, ask. Don't steal. Lesson two: if someone offers you something you need, don't start fixing to argue with him about it!"

By the time I'd tugged the girls into the open, the man was tossing slices of slab bacon to pop and sizzle in the frypan. He broke an egg into the pan, then five more. I hunkered down, nose twitching, staring at that skillet.

The man didn't turn around until they were fried up. The last of his anger leaked away when he saw Maude and Mary. "Two peas in a pod! You ain't bigger than chickadees, much. I got a sister at home just your size." Then he smiled at them. "You two hungry?"

"Yes," Mary said. Maude nodded. Clinging to my hand, she took one step forward, one step back.

"Go on," I said. "It's all right."

The man divvied up the steaming meal into tin cups. Jasper and I pinched up bits of bacon and eggs and popped them in our mouths. "Let it cool," I advised the twins, but couldn't help scooping up another bite. Jasper used his fingers to wipe up every last bit of bacon grease.

"Whooeee," the man said slowly. "I guess you were hungry, all right."

My face grew hot. "Well, we—" I began, but stopped abruptly and pressed a hand against my belly. I shouldn't have eaten so fast. Jasper suddenly darted into the bushes, and I heard him lose the hard-won meal.

The man shook his head. "What are you young'uns doing out on the road by yourselves, anyhow?"

Caution flicked up my spine. "Just traveling."

"You headed far?"

I hesitated. "Nashville. We've got kin there."

The man threw a twig in the fire, his eyebrows coming together in a frown. "Your ma and pa dead?"

"Yes."

"Trouble with the soldiers?"

This was sticky ground. "Yes," I said finally, then added truthfully, "And we had a mule, but a Yankee soldier stole her. We had to leave most of our things by the road."

The young man's hand tightened into a fist, and that fierce anger flamed back in his eyes. "Dag-blame it," he said gruffly. "Those bluebelly Yankee troops come bringing all kinds of trouble. Making war on children. You aren't the first I've seen turned out of house and home, may every Yankee rot in—well, anyway." He tipped his head to one side, as if pondering on something.

Jasper slunk back to join us, wiping his mouth with his sleeve. I fixed him with a warning look: *This man is Confederate.*

The man smacked his fist in his palm. "My name's Willie Spencer. And I'm heading toward Nashville myself. You want to ride along?"

Ride along. To Nashville.

"I mean it," Willie said. "You're welcome to."

Ride along! my heart sang. *With a Confederate sympathizer!* my head scolded. I heard the shots again in my head, the shatter of breaking glass, saw Mama lying still and dead in her bed. "I can't pay," I said finally.

He snorted. "Don't matter. I'm going anyway."

"Well . . ."

He folded his arms. "Look. We got off to a bad start. I know I have a temper, but—"

"You had every right to be mad," I said.

"Thing is, I ain't going to hurt you."

I wiped my palms on my skirt, thinking of a whole new reason I should say no. Mama and Pa had never minded me roaming about with Ben. But Ben was Ben.

"I got little sisters and brothers of my own," Willie added. "I'm hoping if they ever got in such a fix, somebody would lend a helping hand. Besides, you can give me some company. I've been driving for over a week, and I'm about to start talking to myself."

I chewed my lip. Looked at the little ones. Made up my mind.

"All right," I said, wondering if I was shaking hands with the devil. "And thank you. We'll take that ride."

CHAPTER 7

We slept that night curled in our quilts under Willie's wagon, while he wrapped up by the fire. Before going to sleep I had one mighty conversation with Jasper. "I appreciate you trying to take matters in hand and help," I hissed in his ear. "But Camerons do *not* steal. You came close to getting us in a mighty pile of trouble. Don't ever, *ever*, do something like that again."

"I won't. But Hannah, we were out—of—food. And you—"

"I would have found a way. I would have."

"He's a Rebel, you know," Jasper whispered. I didn't know if he was defending his stealing, or worried about trouble.

"I know. But—if he can get us to Nashville . . ." My voice trailed away. I felt like *I* was the one caught stealing.

We spent the next day rumbling east in Willie Spencer's wagon. Sometimes I jounced along amidst barrels of cornmeal and kegs of vinegar and three crates of squawking Barred Rock chickens. The canvas top shielded us from the sun, and I stared out the back, watching the road disappear behind us. Midmorning, Willie paid the ferry toll without blinking an eye, and I watched the far shore fade away as we got hauled across the Caney Fork River.

We took turns sitting on the seat with Willie. "I'm headed to Nashville to sell my goods," he told me. Most farmers sold what they had to sell in autumn, but I nodded, and Willie went on to tell me all about his farm, his brothers and sisters, his mules. He didn't let another traveler pass without a wave and a called greeting. As long as folks treated him right, he was the friendliest, most talky person I'd ever met.

He took a shine to the girls. "What're they saying?" he asked one morning, watching them whispering together.

I shrugged. "They have some language all their own. I've tried to get them to give it up, but they won't." Hearing Maude and Mary use their secret talk made me feel the way I used to when watching Pa and Jasper laugh over some man-folk joke, or seeing Mama's face smooth out like I'd never seen while she talked with Aunt Ellen.

I stared at the girls, remembering when Mama's belly swelled big as a barn, and she told Pa she might be carrying twins. Pa had looked at her for a long moment, then nodded and gone back to oiling his gun. But the next night he started fashioning a second cradle.

Surely one'll be a girl! I'd told myself. I was hungry for a sister—someone special for me, like Aunt Ellen was special for Mama. When the time came, I helped the twins slide into the world. Maude squalled and squirmed. Mary mewed like a runt kitten.

Mama put Maude to sleep in the new cradle, and Mary in the old. "You and Jasper grew strong in that cradle," she whispered. But as the days ticked past, Maude grew and Mary faded. One evening Pa reached a callused hand toward Mary, then drew it back. "They both could have fit in one cradle," he said to Mama, with a fierce swipe at his eyes. "Don't give that one your heart."

I watched Mama and Pa leaning together, giving comfort to each other. Then I took Maude from her blankets and gently eased her into the old cradle beside Mary. Maude had rested one tiny hand on Mary's belly. And from that moment Mary had begun to get stronger.

"What are you thinking about?" Willie asked.

"Oh!" I shook my head to clear it. "The twins. I was just thinking how Mary's always tended toward sickly. I've been worried about her something terrible." I looked him in the eye. "She's doing better since we hitched up with you." I could see the difference already—a bit of color in her thin cheeks.

"Good. She's tiny as a wren. And that one sure is a shy little thing," he said, watching Maude carefully spoon a bite of oatmeal.

"She wasn't always," I managed. "But I haven't heard her laugh in ever so long."

That evening Willie taught Jasper and Mary and Maude how to play a game he'd made up—something to do with tossing pebbles into a row of circles marked in the dirt. When Maudie did well he said, "Nicely done there!" Maude rewarded him with a shy smile, and he grinned at me over her head.

That night Willie slept out by the fire again. I was watchful, but Willie acted like he didn't notice when the twins and I went off to the bushes to relieve ourselves. And he stayed well away once we'd bedded down, even when it drizzled rain and he had to roll up in a gum blanket.

We all tried to help out with chores, fetching firewood and harnessing his mules, but Willie usually pitched in so quick himself there wasn't much left to do. So I was pleased when, on our third evening on the road together, Willie asked me for help with supper. "Pop back to the wagon, will you, Hannah?" He was kneeling by the new-made fire and paused to carefully blow a tiny finger of flame to life amongst the tinder. "There's a crock of my ma's raspberry preserves packed in a crate. That'd go well with supper."

I didn't have any trouble finding the crock of preserves, sealed with beeswax and packed in sawdust. Raspberry preserves! I could have sat down with a spoon and finished off the whole crock by myself.

I started to climb back out of the wagon but noticed that a basket of young turnips had spilled. We'd jounced over some mighty ruts that day—no doubt that had pitched 'em over. "This whole place needs a good cleaning," I muttered, looking around the jumbled wagon.

I peeked around the canvas cover to see if Willie was waiting on me, but he was still fussing with the fire. The little ones wandered about nearby, gathering wood. I had time to do a spot of cleaning.

I was almost finished when I noticed the oddest thing—an

egg had somehow rolled behind a little barrel of vinegar in the corner and gotten wedged. No telling how long that'd been there! I couldn't quite reach it, so I had to wrestle that barrel over a bit. I rescued the egg and put it aside. But before I could shove the barrel back in place I noticed something else odd. One of the floorboards had popped up an inch or so once the barrel's weight had been pulled away. But I didn't see daylight below the loose board.

Frowning, I pulled it up a bit farther. It wasn't nailed down at all! And it wasn't a true floorboard. There was something underneath—

Guns. A mess of 'em, packed together in an empty space beneath the false bed, polished stocks and gleaming barrels—

The hand that clamped around my arm like to broke the bone. "*What are you doing?*" Willie growled, and jerked me so hard I fell against the tailboard and cracked my knee. He was standing on the ground behind the wagon.

"Nothing! I—"

"You lying little sneak!" He swung himself into the wagon. "You were spying! Who sent you after me? *Who?*"

"Nobody!" I tried to scramble away but there was nowhere to go. I scrunched down beside a crate. "Nobody, I swear!"

Willie was crouched tight as a panther ready to spring. "Then what were you doing poking around in here?"

"An egg," I babbled. "Cleaning—I just thought to tidy up— I wanted to surprise you, and I saw an egg that had rolled behind the barrel, and I couldn't reach it, and—"

"And where is this egg?" His voice was rough as a corncob.

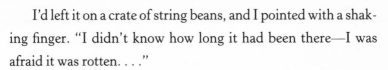

I'd left it on a crate of string beans, and I pointed with a shaking finger. "I didn't know how long it had been there—I was afraid it was rotten. . . ."

He picked up the egg, the iron look never leaving my face. Then he leaned over the wagon's backboard and smashed the egg against the wood panel.

A sudden stink choked off the soft night air. The egg was rotten. Thank the Lord, it was rotten.

Willie stared at the mess on his hand. His shoulders sagged, and he pulled out a kerchief to wipe his fingers. It took him a moment to meet my eye. "I'm sorry, Hannah," he said finally.

"It's . . . it's all right," I lied. He'd spooked at least a year off my life. Maybe two.

"Hey, Willie, we're about ready—" Jasper appeared at the back of the wagon. His cheer faded when he saw my face. "What's wrong?" he demanded.

"Nothing," Willie said. "Go back by the fire and wait for us."

Jasper looked to me. "Run on," I told him. "We'll be there in a minute." He went slowly, looking back over his shoulder.

I wanted nothing more than to creep out of the wagon and follow, but Willie wasn't done yet. "You deserve an explanation," he said slowly. "Can you keep a secret?"

I swallowed hard.

He knocked on the wagon's floor. "It's a false bed. I'm running a load of muskets and rifles to our army. Selling goods is just my story."

I wanted to plug my ears with my fingers. "That right?" I said, sounding weak as a sick pup.

Willie must have seen my look. "Now, I'm not trying to scare you. But you're old enough to know what's going on. Good Tennessee men don't aim to allow those Yankees to just march in here prim as you please. We've made all kinds of plans. Your own pa is gone, I know. But I want you to understand that there's plenty of men left to protect you, and fight for what's right. That's why I'm telling you this."

"It's—it's good to know."

Willie finished wiping his fingers and dropped the kerchief out of the wagon. "Now, don't worry on it. I don't expect any trouble. If it should come, you lie low in the wagon." Then he went back out to cook supper, cheerful as you please. I had to sit for a while before I felt ready to follow.

That night Jasper poked me in the ribs. "What was going on in the wagon?" he whispered.

"Nothing."

"Hannah—"

"I said nothing!" I hissed, and rolled away from him.

Every day we sat in Willie's wagon as it lurched and rumbled closer to Nashville, and every day we ate the food he cooked for us. Thinking about what Willie didn't know about us twisted my belly into knots, and thinking about his guns brought goose bumps to my skin. But after all the painful miles we'd walked, Willie still seemed like a heaven-sent miracle.

We passed more and more people during those days—trudging along the road, driving wagons and carts, sometimes camped under tattered quilts and scraps of canvas, sacks of cornmeal and pieces of heirloom silver piled all a-tumble in baskets and trunks. One afternoon I was sitting on the wagon seat while Willie talked about hogs. "My pa always lets 'em forage until butchering. The flavor is just middling, and the meat is greasy and loose. I figure, if you bring 'em in a month or so before, and feed 'em on slops and a fist or so of corn, it'll firm up the meat. . . ."

We rattled out of a stand of woods and around a bend. A field met the tree line—hard-won, with some stumps and trees still standing amongst the corn. I could see a frame house in the distance, with a barn beyond. But on my side of the road, in a lit-tle grassy spot a ways up the fencerow, a mule and cart was parked. I recognized that rig.

Ben's sister, Sary, was sitting in the grass, knees drawn up, face hidden. Behind her, Ben was piling rocks on a long, low mound. My stomach dropped with a sickening lurch.

It was a new-made grave.

Ben slowly placed one stone on the grave, just so. Then he walked heavily back to the edge of the cornfield, where the farmer had piled rocks pitched from the field into a cairn, and picked up another.

". . . and my ma said the lard from that pig was the sweetest she ever saw," Willie said, "and I told her it was because we'd cut all the acorns from the grub. . . ."

I remembered how peaked Ben's mother had looked the last time I'd seen her. I gripped the edge of the wagon seat hard, turning my head to stare as the wagon rumbled past. I knew how it felt to shovel dirt on your own mother's grave.

At the last second Ben looked up. He stared, and I stared,

and in that moment I felt that he still knew me better than anyone else. My insides felt all quivery. And then the wagon went
past, and Ben was gone from view.

"... so my pa said next fall, he'll give it a try, and I do think it
will go better." Willie paused to wave a pesky fly away. "I figure—"

"Willie, stop!"

"Whoa, there." Willie reined in, set the brake, and fixed me
with a look of surprise. "What's the matter?"

I was already scrambling down from the tall seat. I ran back
toward the grave, then slowed. Stopped. I didn't know what to
say. Ben turned from picking up a rock and saw me standing
there like a scarecrow. Mud caked his britches, and his linen
shirt was torn at one elbow. I would have given Willie's wagon
for a needle and thread right then.

A jay landed on the fence rail and began to scold. "What
do you want?" Ben asked finally, then added the stone to his
mother's grave.

"I just thought—"

Sary raised her head sharply. "Go on with you!" she sobbed.
"We don't want you here."

Willie caught up with me. "Oh Lordy," he said, looking at
the grave. "I'm surely sorry. Can we help? How about—"

"We don't need any help from the likes of you," Ben told
him. His voice sounded like a plank of oak. Hard. Flat.

"The likes of . . ." Willie sounded confused.

My palms got sticky-damp. Lord Almighty. Ben surely
thought Willie was a Unionist. I glanced at my brother and sisters, watching wide-eyed from the back of the wagon.

"Look, now," Willie tried, "you two can't stay out here on your own. I've got food, I can give you a ride—"

"I said we don't need any help!" Ben stepped closer to Sary and put a hand on her shoulder. *Family.*

Willie finally gave up. I lingered just long enough to get another good scolding from that blue jay. Then I turned my back too.

"I hate to see such a sight," Willie muttered as he snapped the lines again. "Bluebelly Yankees, bringing this curse on Tennessee. . . ."

I hung on to the seat as the wagon lurched forward, thinking about the guns hidden in this very wagon. Thinking about Pa. Thinking about Ben. I wished mightily for that heart of stone Preacher had talked of—one that couldn't feel anything.

"There will be the devil to pay. There surely will. Don't you think so, Hannah?"

"I guess," I mumbled, but my mind was back in that grassy spot, beside that grave. *Stones.* I remembered Ben laughing as he skipped stones on the creek, and the look in his eyes when he'd given me the gray hearthstone like a promise. I remembered him throwing a fury of stones at us. But those memories all faded against the picture of Ben placing those stones on his mother's grave. At least my mama rested in our own soil.

I didn't know what Ben and Sary were headed to. But I sure hoped they found it all right.

Traffic on that road was getting mighty thick. We got slowed quite a bit as buggies and grain wagons and coaches bickered for space. Once a Union Army wagon train rumbled past, shoving everyone else aside. I dared a glance at Willie. I felt about ready to explode. Willie talked to his mules and picked his nails and acted like running guns past Union Army soldiers was something he did 'most every day. Maybe it was.

The Union troops disappeared before I figured out what to do. I told myself there really wasn't any way I could turn Willie in without maybe bringing trouble down on us too. What if shooting started? I couldn't put the twins and Jasper smack in the middle of a brawl, could I?

Late that afternoon Willie stopped at a pretty farm and asked a sour-faced woman if he could buy some fresh food. Before he was through we had a new-butchered chicken and a nice melon and a jug full of milk, still warm from the udder. Willie paid for the food and split the woman some wood, and had that woman laughing by the time he climbed back to the seat and drove away.

"Willie, you sure are nice to folks," I said while he waved to the woman disappearing behind us.

"Well, sure!" He sounded surprised. "Why not? Most folks are nice back."

I wasn't quite as sure. "Anyway . . . you've been more than nice to us. I don't know how I'd have managed. We were about done in."

He grinned. "I've been glad for the company. Don't think on it. Think on how you want that chicken instead. Stewed? Or maybe fried?"

Willie found a campsite that evening near a nice spring.

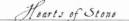

Quick as a summer storm, we had firewood gathered and a blaze going, the chicken plucked and gutted and in the stewpot. With the melon and a little rice, it made a fine meal.

Once he'd eaten, Jasper was even feeling brass enough to climb a big oak tree while I washed up the dishes. "I want to find out if I can see Nashville," he announced. He couldn't, so he perched on one of the strong lower limbs, tossing acorns and twigs at Mary. Maude was collecting leaves. I smiled.

"Look at me!" Jasper yelled. Sitting on the limb, holding on, he swung backwards until he was hanging from his knees, his arms dangling down in the air. "Look—"

Something fell to the ground—several somethings, as his pockets emptied. I scrambled to my feet. But Willie was closer, and soon had the objects in his hand: a whittling knife, a spare button. And two tintypes.

His smile faded.

Jasper scrambled down. He took one look at Willie's face and came to stand beside me. I couldn't help grabbing his shoulder, giving a shake. "How could you have been so careless?" I cried, then shoved him behind me, away from Willie. "Girls, come here," I commanded, and when they came, I shoved them behind Jasper and me.

Willie hadn't moved. My mouth went dry. Jasper stealing from him, me finding those guns . . . this would surely be too much. Willie was a good fellow who could not *abide* being crossed.

Lord Almighty.

"Run," I muttered, and Maude and Mary took off like shots.

But my legs had turned to wood, and although I could feel Jasper twitching, he stayed put too.

Finally Willie raised his head. "Is this your pa?" he asked, in a rusty voice.

I opened my mouth and nothing came out. The lump in my throat felt like a stone. Finally I nodded.

"He was a Yankee soldier?"

I nodded again.

Willie came toward us and I put my arms up, expecting him to pull his pistol—or at least hit me. But he didn't. "I trusted you with my secrets, Hannah," he said. "Seems the least you could have done was trust me with yours." He pushed the images into my hand. "Put these away someplace safe." Then he walked away, disappearing around the wagon.

annah, why did Willie say he'd still take us to Nashville?" Jasper whispered to me that night. We were curled into our blankets beneath the wagon. The girls were already asleep. Willie sat out by the fire, just staring. "Isn't he angry at us?"

"I think more than that, we hurt his feelings, letting him think we were for the Confederacy."

"I thought he'd hurt us, sure as you're born."

"Me too, for a minute." I sighed. I almost wished Willie *had* gotten angry.

Jasper rolled onto his back. "I wish that Jack fellow had been so nice. Him being in the Union Army like Papa and all."

"I guess . . . I guess there's good and bad in both armies. On both sides." I wondered if Ben knew that. I wondered how he and Sary were faring.

"I suppose." Jasper sounded low too.

The night air smelled damp. A whip-poor-will began to call. After a while I sighed. "It's more than that. I think Jack didn't all-the-way want to take Star. Maybe back home, before the war, he was a nice fellow too."

"You think?"

"Truth is, I'm trying mightily hard not to think at all. Go to sleep, Jasper."

"But—"

"Go to sleep!" I rolled over, so if Jasper had any more talking to do, he'd be aimed at my back. Mary slept on my other side. I listened to her breathe, fragile as a spiderweb. Maude lay beyond, with her tin cup and spoon hugged close even in sleep. It took me a long time to go to sleep that night.

Willie fed us, and drove us on to the city, and never said one mean word. But he didn't laugh or tell stories anymore. I shouldn't feel bad! I told myself over and over. He's running Rebel guns! I'd done the best I could to protect Jasper and Maude and Mary.

But it was still hard to look Willie in the eye.

He said good-bye just outside Nashville. "Sorry I can't take you all the way in, but I'd have to pass through the Union sentries. I can't risk it."

"We're fine. I can't thank you enough for what you've done," I mumbled.

He frowned, squinting at the sky. "Looks like it could rain. Smells like it too."

"We'll be fine," I said again, hoping it was true.

"Take care of the others, Hannah." Willie hesitated. "And let me give you some advice." I nodded, waiting to hear about the glory of Southern independence. Instead, he pointed at my top button. "I don't know what you're wearing under there, but don't touch it so much. Don't touch it at all. There are a lot of thieves in a big place like Nashville."

Mama's wedding ring with the green stone still hung around my neck on its piece of string. "I won't," I said. "Thank you."

Then Willie climbed back to his wagon seat, and clucked at his mules, and edged back into the traffic. I watched him go, angry at myself for feeling so lost.

Nashville perched on a bluff overlooking the Cumberland River. The Union sentry post Willie had worried about turned out to be a couple of soldiers in blue uniforms posted at the turn-pike. They were stopping anybody riding or in a wagon or buggy—which caused lots of shouting, something about need-ing a pass—but a river of people on foot just swerved into a muddy field by the road and flowed right on by.

"Well, here we are," I said finally. My voice sounded puny.

"You got us here, sure enough," Jasper allowed.

That was all he said, but it shored me up some.

We trudged into Nashville with some fried-up bacon and corn cakes—final gifts from Willie—wrapped in a piece of cloth. We put on our shoes and washed best we could in a horse trough, and I plaited the girls' hair with fingers suddenly all a-tremble. I hoped we wouldn't put fright into Aunt Ellen.

We passed some big places belching smoke with signs like BRENNAN'S FOUNDRY and DINGLE'S BRICKYARD. When we got past them and into the city proper, the streets narrowed, and the crush of traffic got even worse. "Hold my hand," I ordered Mary. Maude was already clinging to my skirt like a wood tick.

"Did you ever imagine so many buildings?" Jasper was gawking. We passed all kinds, crushed up against one another: brick, frame, some log. Some were taller than I thought safe, all those bricks stacked up one on another, with windows in three, four, even five stories. There was also a fancy white place up ahead on a hill that looked like it might have been fit for heavenly angels except Yankee soldiers had fixed some big guns up there.

"What's that?" Mary asked, pointing to a tall iron pole with a glass cage on top.

"I don't know."

Jasper grabbed his nose. "Crimus, Hannah! What is that stink?"

"I—I think it's the roads." Garbage and enormous piles of horse droppings, buzzing with flies, littered streets jammed with supply wagons, buggies filled with ladies wearing fine bonnets, carts pushed by men selling fish and cabbage, even a string of bawling beef cattle being herded past. First time we came to a crossing it took me quite a while to scrape up the backbone to drag the others into the street. We scuttled across like crawdads.

We came to bricks laid down in paths to walk on. I'd never seen so many people: white women in ragged clothing carrying babies, black women hauling baskets of laundry. Fancy ladies in enormous belled skirts that like to shove us off the walkways, men in plaid wool vests and dark sack coats hurrying past. On 'most every corner, somebody was bellowing about something for sale—peaches from little carts or eggs from baskets. One old woman with no teeth

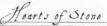

had an apron full of blackberries. She sold by the handful, and folks walked on munching and licking their fingers.

"Almighty," I whispered. Why had I ever thought we should come here? A body couldn't live, couldn't think or breathe, in all this noise and crush—

"Hannah, ow!" Maude yelped. I'd been squeezing her hand too tight. She looked as scared as I felt. I would have given an acre of good flatland to be safe back in the mountains, even if it meant hoeing corn for Preacher Peabody and his wife for the rest of my days.

Then I heard someone whistling "The Ploughboy." I whirled around, sure it was Ben, but it was a young Yankee with shocking red hair. I swallowed hard, then touched Mama's ring, just once. At least my folks had been for the Union. How was Ben faring among so many Union soldiers? Yankee messengers galloped through the crowded streets bellowing "Make way! Make way!" as they passed. Bunches of Yankee men stomped past in columns. A block or two farther we passed a passel of sweating Yankees, stripped to their blouses and whacking away with axes at several mighty oak trees in front of a grand-looking building. An angry crowd seemed more than a mite displeased with the soldiers for turning the city's fine old trees into firewood.

"Where does Aunt Ellen live?" Mary asked. Her eyes were wide.

"Cherry Street." I had memorized the name. "But I have to ask where that is."

A Union soldier with fancy gold bars on the shoulders of his uniform stopped nearby to pull a gold watch on a chain from his pocket. I sucked in a deep breath and stepped closer. "Excuse me, sir?"

"Yes? What is it?" The soldier snapped the gold watch shut and dangled the chain. "Are you orphans? You have to report to the refugee asylum."

I didn't know what a refugee asylum was, and didn't want to find out. "Please, sir, where is Cherry Street? We're trying to find our aunt Ellen."

"Oh, you're just lost, are you?" He seemed relieved. "Cherry Street is a few blocks that way." He pointed, giving directions. He pronounced some of his words funny, but I listened as best I could before thanking him.

It took us longer than I expected to find Cherry Street. I dragged the others past a fat man cracking a whip for no particular reason I could divine. We passed several rows of stores that seemed to sell just one thing, ladies' hats or cigars or candy and such. Whole stores, just for candy! Sometimes we passed food stores and could see pickle barrels or piles of yams inside, and I'd pull the others along before their noses got pressed to the windows.

"Hannah, let's eat the bacon and corn cakes," Jasper said finally. "I'm hungry."

"I think we should save those to give Aunt Ellen," I said. I hated the idea of arriving with empty hands. Besides, my own stomach was churning fit to make butter.

By the time we found Cherry Street I felt turned inside out. I approached the nearest house, a gray frame building that needed paint, and knocked on the door. After a moment a tired-looking

woman in a shapeless dress appeared, and I heard a squalling baby from somewhere inside. "I'm looking for Ellen Johnston," I began. "Do you know her—"

"No," the woman said, and slammed the door.

Cherry Street stretched a long way, right through the center of town. There, fine big houses stared from behind iron fences, and I learned quick enough to knock on back doors, for servants to answer. "You think Aunt Ellen lives in a house like these?" Jasper asked, his voice full of wonderment.

"Well, maybe Aunt Ellen works for some rich folks."

But we didn't find her at one of those fancy places, and Cherry Street faded back into a skinny lane where shabby little houses leaned one against another. Jasper started holding his nose again against the stink of manure and boiled cabbage and whatever else hung in the sticky air. Most of the buildings here had rented rooms, so each house had five or six inside doors to knock on. I knocked and knocked and knocked. No one had ever heard of Ellen Johnston.

And then I found someone who didn't shake her head. "Ellen Johnston? She used to live across the hall," said an elderly woman hugging a plaid wool shawl around her shoulders with painfully gnarled fingers.

I wanted to whoop with happiness. This lady knew Aunt Ellen!

Then the words pounded home. "*Used* to?" I squeezed Mary's hand so hard she jerked it away. "She's our aunt, you see, and—"

The woman pulled the shawl a little tighter. "I'm sorry," she whispered. "She's dead."

CHAPTER 9

I stared at her. Then a man's angry voice cut the air: "Ma? Who is it?"

"It was fever," the woman murmured. "About . . . six weeks ago. I'm sorry." She backed into her room.

I might have stared at that closed door for a long time if the man inside hadn't started yelling at his mother. I bolted. Once outside I leaned against the wall of that grimy building, but my knees wouldn't hold. I slid down in a heap.

"Aunt Ellen's dead?" Mary whispered, her lips puckering.

Jasper grabbed my arm. "What do we do now? You said we'd be all right in Nashville! It was your idea to come here!"

I pressed both fists against my mouth like a dam.

"We should never have left home!" Jasper's voice was so loud that an old woman shuffling past with a basket of potatoes on her arm turned to stare. *"Hannah—"*

"I *know!*" Everything I'd crammed inside shoved out like a flood. "But it's *not* my fault! It's Aunt Ellen's fault for dying. And Mama's for dying. And Papa's for leaving and dying—"

"Hannah Cameron, that's wicked!" Jasper gasped.

"Mama didn't die a'purpose," Maude whimpered.

I balled my hands in my skirt. "Mama always said family is everything, but she was *wrong*. Family don't mean a hill of butter beans if your pa marches off and everybody dies. That slave woman and Willie the Confederate treated us better than our own neighbors and kin and the Yankees have, and that's the g-gospel truth!" I drew up my knees, buried my head in my arms, and cried until I had to stop—not because I felt any better, but because I was out of tears.

Finally I raised my head, wiping my cheeks with a shaking hand. A man pushing a two-wheeled cart trundled past, yelling "Fresh fish! Fresh fish!" The world wasn't going to stop just because I didn't have a notion what to do next.

I sniffed hard and wiped my nose on my sleeve. "Jasper, y-you were ri-right," I managed. My voice still had the shudders from crying so hard. "We should ne-never have left home. We should have turned back when Jack stole Star. This mess is my fault. No one else's."

Jasper hitched his shoulders up and down. "I don't know, Hannah." He sighed. "You didn't know Aunt Ellen was dead."

"I was being muleheaded."

"Well . . . I figure you made the best choice you could. I'm sorry I hollered at you."

"Really?" I shoved away one last tear.

"Really."

Mary patted my arm. "It will be all right, Hannah," she echoed soberly, and Maude nodded. "You'll think of something."

I had a funny, *nothing* kind of feeling inside. Even the brambles that had squeezed my heart for so long were gone. "Let's get moving," I said finally.

As we walked back toward the center of town, the gray clouds let loose a drizzle. I noticed more people who didn't seem to have a home. Black folks and white. Some were walking too, dragging blanket rolls or lumpy canvas bags. But some had faded back amongst the darkest alleys and hidden places, like woodworms among barn boards. They'd stretched scraps of quilts over crates and bits of lumber. Hollow-eyed children huddled underneath . . . and their mothers.

I rubbed Mama's ring. I purely couldn't help it.

Then I picked a camp where someone had made a windbreak by dragging a big wooden sign beneath the shelter of an outdoor stairway on the back of a butcher shop. I tipped my head and made out, among the cracked paint, MISS TEMPLE, FINE SEWING, and I wondered what had happened to Miss Temple, and if she was crouched in some smelly alley too. Behind the sign two girls in faded homespun dresses slept on a blanket. A hatchet-faced woman was pegging socks on a bit of string.

"Excuse me, ma'am," I began. "Do you mind if we—"

"Git!" The woman was on her feet before I could finish my sentence, waving us off like stray dogs. "Git on with you!"

The twins ran halfway back down the alley. I tried again. "I just wanted to make a place to rest a spell beside you."

But the woman would have none of it. "Go on!" she cried, raising a fist. "I found this spot plain and fair! I won't have you all sneaking in on us!"

"Well, fine!" I cried, and stomped away. I didn't dare argue anymore. The woman had a look in her eye like our old sow protecting new piglets. I had never crossed our old sow, and I knew better than to cross this woman now. I didn't know how to explain that I didn't want to take her shelter, or share whatever food she had. What I had really wanted, I guess, was to have someone to peg out *my* socks on a bit of string while I slept on a blanket.

Well, it wasn't to be. I picked up Mary, who had sunk to the road, and squeezed Jasper's shoulder. "Come along. Forget about her."

"Let's find a place of our own," Jasper said. He took Maude's hand.

I looked at the sun, then turned my head east toward Cumberland Mountain. I wanted to start walking east. Start walking *home*. But for the moment, I needed another plan.

We could at least leave the dark, stinking alleys behind. I led the others downhill to the wharf area beside the Cumberland River. It wasn't a clean, tumbling river like those we knew at home, but a big sleepy, smelly thing with a clarty yellow look to it. Four or five big riverboats were lined up along the bank, neat as cows in their own stalls. Several were still and empty. One had presses of people lined along the railings, and a line of more passengers huddled beneath umbrellas and shiny black oilskin waiting to climb aboard, while the black smokestacks coughed smoke and cinders over everything.

Jasper stopped. "Where do you suppose those boats are headed?"

"I don't know." I sighed. "And I don't much care."

The riverbank sloped real gentle toward the steamboats, and planks stretched the rest of the way on board. Sweating men were unloading one boat, straining under barrels and crates like oxen straining from the plow, those planks bouncing with every step. A bit away from the riverfront was a row of tall warehouses, all crushed together. In the muddy space between, teamsters swore, men in little blue caps shouted orders, hunched merchants counted stacks of crates and kegs and made tick marks in their ledgers. Haulers edged their carts among the traffic, bellowing, "Make way! Get on there!"

And two boys hawked newspapers nearby, each trying to outshout the other. "*Nashville Dispatch!*" the first yelled, and the other scowled and yelled, "*Nashville Daily Union!,*" which just set the first to shouting even louder.

Of course. That was the answer.

First things first. We edged through until we'd left most of the ruckus behind. The drizzle didn't show any signs of letting up. The day was fading. I had to find some shelter, and soon. In a quiet yard near a big warehouse I saw stacks of railroad ties and thought about fixing a little hidey-hole, but they were too heavy to move. We wandered a bit farther among the stacked cargo, and suddenly I caught sight of a huge coil of rope. It was bigger around than any rope I'd ever seen before, and coiled almost as high as Jasper's head.

I put Mary down and untied my blanket roll. "Here's home, for the night." And hoped to my bones that none of them would pitch a fit about it, because I didn't know what I'd do then. I purely didn't know.

Maude hung back. "In there?"

I kissed the top of her head. "Yes, Maudie, in there. We'll stretch our oilcloth over the top. We'll be a bit cramped, but we can stay dry. All right?" Jasper opened his mouth, looked at my face, closed it again. "Just for tonight," I added.

I took the girls around a pile of railroad ties and spread my skirt while the girls relieved themselves. Then I hoisted them into the coil of rope. Jasper scrambled in after them. I followed, managing to upset the top few coils, but the rope was so heavy it didn't move much. Jasper and I stretched our oilcloth overhead, tucking the ends in beneath the top layer of rope. Our first effort snugged us in good, but it was pitch-dark and hard to breathe. After a bit more trial we fixed it so we still had a little hole, on the downwind side of the rain.

After we got settled, everybody was quiet for a spell. Finally, Jasper sighed, "Oh, Hannah. What are we going to do?"

"We're going to have supper." I doled out the bacon and corn cakes Willie had given us, and passed around the jar of water. Jasper lit into his, but neither girl did more than nibble.

"Maude, Mary, I have something else for you." I unfolded the piece of wool tartan and pulled out the little rag doll. "There now, see? Something from Mama."

"Oh!" Maude gasped. "I thought she was gone!" She took the tattered, dirty doll like a sacred thing. A smile lit Mary's face.

They murmured something to each other and finished their meal with Dolly nestled between them.

I gave Jasper my last piece of bacon. "You have it. I'm not hungry," I lied, and he gobbled it down. I pressed the tartan against my cheek. That was my gift to me.

Then I announced my plan. "Tomorrow, I'm going to look for work."

"What kind of work?" Jasper asked.

"I don't know," I admitted. "But I'll find something."

"I can work too," Jasper said stoutly.

"We both can. Did you see those boys selling newspapers? They weren't any older than you. Maybe younger."

"How do you get newspapers to sell?"

"I guess find the place that prints the newspapers, and see if they need more help."

I couldn't see Jasper's face in the gloom, but he sounded brighter. "Tomorrow morning. We'll go first thing."

"First thing." I nodded. If Jasper or I could find work—something that would let one of us keep an eye on the twins—we'd make out. "We'll be all right. We'll get work, and make money, and save it until we have enough to get us back home." I wasn't ready to figure out how much money we would need to get us back home. "Let's try to get some sleep."

I was too tired to sing, and nobody asked me to. Maude and Mary curled into a ball, hugging Dolly. Jasper and I sat against the coils, knees bent, feet jammed against the rope across from us. It was cramped. Coils dug into my back even with my quilt shoved between. I was damp, and still hungry.

But at least we were together.

Sleep was a long time in coming. And while I waited for it, hearing every strange sound, every distant shout and dog's howl, I found myself thinking of Ben. Were he and Sary hungry, and scared, and looking for a place to sleep too?

If Ben was in Nashville, I knew he was as miserable as I was. Ben needed space and quiet and green. He liked seeing otters belly-slip down their muddy slides, and guessing how fireflies flashed their yellow-green lights, and watching waterthrushes. "Most birds hop," he'd pointed out once, "but waterthrushes walk on their two feet. Why do you suppose that is?" And we'd pondered that for quite a spell.

"Ben," I finally asked, "do you figure there's a way to find answers for such things?"

"Maybe," he said. We were lying on our bellies, watching a waterthrush wander among the moss and wintergreen growing beside the McNeills' springhouse.

"In books, do you suppose?"

"Maybe," he'd allowed. "But I think if you just watch the world, and think about it, little by little it starts to make sense."

"Wrong again," I muttered now. And finally, I fell asleep.

CHAPTER 10

hen we scrambled out at first light I was stiff as a willow whistle, and just as hollow.

"Hannah, I'm hungry," Maude whimpered as we rolled up our things.

"So am I," I said, as even as I could.

People were already about, bumping through the gray light: farm folks come into the city with fresh eggs and crocks of butter, storekeepers buying it from them, draymen clattering past with wagons loaded and bound for one of the steamships.

We found the newspaper buildings, but at each a man—one short and barrel-chested, one tall and skinny as a new sapling—said they weren't hiring. After that we knocked on door after door. I offered to scrub floors, to sew men's shirts, to help stitch soles to shiny leather shoes. Jasper offered to help a wheelwright, a cooper, a blacksmith. It was the same everywhere.

By the time the sun was high overhead, I felt light-headed. The children plodded along ahead of me with slumped shoulders. "We'll find work soon," I promised, but no one responded.

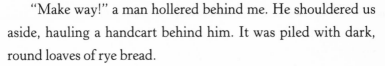

"Make way!" a man hollered behind me. He shouldered us aside, hauling a handcart behind him. It was piled with dark, round loaves of rye bread.

My hand shot out, grabbed a loaf, and buried it under my apron.

The peddler trudged on without turning his head, snapping at more people to make way. My brother and sisters let him pass, then began to walk again. I was frozen. My heart banged in my chest. The tiny hairs on my arms prickled. I waited for the hand of God, or Mama, or Pa, to strike me down. I waited for someone on the street to point a finger in my face, shouting, "Thief! Thief!"

Instead two old women glared at me because they had to pass on either side. After a moment Jasper glanced back and stopped. He called to the twins, and they retraced their steps. "What's wrong?" Jasper asked, looking worried.

The peddler turned a corner and disappeared. I tried to speak and nothing came out. I swallowed hard and tried again. "Come into the alley." I jerked my head.

"But—"

"Just *come!*"

I shoved the little ones close in front of me. With my back to the street, I slipped the little loaf free. The ash-covered crust made it difficult to break the loaf into even pieces. It must have been baked in a brick bakeoven.

"Where did you get that?" Jasper demanded.

"Just eat it."

"*Hannah!*" Jasper stared from the bread in his hand to me. "Hannah Cameron!"

"I mean it, Jasper. Just hush your mouth and eat it. You too, girls. I don't want to hear another word."

Huddled like gossips, we ate. The stolen bread tasted of rye and molasses. Maybe even a hint of caraway. The soft part was heavy and moist on my tongue. The crust crunched between my teeth. I thought it might choke in my throat, or ball sour in my stomach. But it didn't. It tasted *fine*.

Well, I thought. Now I am a thief. I remembered Pa standing square to say his prayers, facing the Lord. Well.

All too quickly the last crumb was gone. "Come along," I said briskly, and led the others back to the street.

The afternoon passed as the morning had. Someone told us a pin maker wanted children to put heads on pins, but after tramping halfway across the city, he said he wasn't hiring. The pin maker told us to try an umbrella maker who sometimes hired girls to sew the silk over the frames, but he wasn't hiring either. The umbrella maker said Jasper might get hired by the army men at the Franklin Shops south of the city, or the smelly city tannery on Nolensville Pike. He didn't.

No one had any work. "There's a thousand like you in Nashville," one man at a furniture shop said sadly. "I can't help you."

By then I was very hungry again. I will *not* steal anymore, I vowed, but panic bubbled up in my chest. I clenched and unclenched my fists, trying to think. Just ahead was a large general store. "Come on," I said, and we climbed the steps.

When I pushed the door open, smells slapped me: pickles in brine, musty potatoes a bit too long in storage, sour yeast bread. A couple of new-butchered chickens hung by their ankles in one

corner. Glass jars of lemon drops and horehound candy sparkled on the counter. This grocer stocked a bit of everything, although some of his shelves were dusty-bare. A big, hand-lettered sign was posted behind the counter: NO CREDIT.

"Can I help you young folks?" the man behind the counter asked. He looked to be maybe ten years older than me, with dark hair that grew down his cheeks in bushy side-whiskers.

"Please, sir, do you have any work?" I put a hand on a barrel of soda crackers to steady myself.

"Sorry, I—"

"*Please*," I interrupted. "I'll do anything. Clean, or—or unpack, or whatever you need. You don't have to pay money. Just a little food . . . ." My voice got scrawny, so I stopped talking.

But he shook his head. "You've got to clear out. I can't have—" He was interrupted when a little bell tinkled over the door, and a broomstick-thin woman came in, market basket over her arm. "Off with you!" the storekeeper hissed at us.

I didn't have it in me to move. We stood in a corner like hungry hounds at a church picnic, watching him reach for what the woman wanted. Two sweet potatoes. A bit of molasses. Four pickled pigs' feet from a barrel.

"And one of those straw fans," the woman said, pointing to several plaited straw fans high on one of the back corner shelves. I'd seen Mama make some just like it after threshing was done.

I hadn't noticed the crutch leaning against the wall until the storekeeper snugged it in place and hobbled from behind the counter. At the bottom of his left trouser leg was . . . nothing. His foot was missing. The storekeeper picked up a long, thin stick and tried to tap one of the fans free. "My apologies, Mrs. Hamilton," he grunted. "Just give me a moment—"

"No apologies needed," the woman said, shaking her head. "Your sacrifice at First Manassas will not be forgotten by the Confederacy, Mr. Norton."

First Manassas. I recalled hearing of a battle fought at such a place. He must have lost his foot there. I shoved aside my pity and dragged the others over to Mr. Norton. "Jasper, help me heft Mary up," I grunted. They caught on quick. In two shakes Mary had one of those fans down.

Mr. Norton took it with a hard look. But while he figured up the woman's order, I pulled my apron off and gave it to Mary. "Climb back up there and dust off those high shelves," I whispered. "Maude, dust this lower bit. Jasper, see if you can find a bucket and broom."

Mr. Norton waited until after the woman had left before turning on us. "Now look here," he growled. "I told you—"

"I'm just doing you a Christian turn," I told him. "We've got no place to go and nothing to do, and your store here could use a bit of cleaning up. I'm sure you could do it yourself," I added, when his scowl got meaner. "But you being so busy with customers and all, I just figured we might help you with some of the tricky bits."

Before he could holler, the bell dingled again. When he turned to the customer I slid into a back storeroom and found a couple of dirty cleaning rags, a bucket, and broom.

"There's a pump out back," Jasper reported, sticking his head out the door.

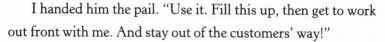

I handed him the pail. "Use it. Fill this up, then get to work out front with me. And stay out of the customers' way!"

We all lit to it like Mama on the first sunny day of spring. We swept and washed and dusted. Jasper removed an old mouse nest from a faded ladies' bonnet on one of the high shelves. I climbed up on a chair to dust even the forgotten merchandise on another set of shelves, little pots that said MRS. BENNINGTON'S SALVE and a cracked lamp chimney and cards of bone buttons and such.

Mr. Norton shot us stormy looks, but customers came in and out, keeping him busy. A woman with red cheeks bought a sack of snuff. An old man bought a peppermint stick. Another old man brought in a basket of smelly glassy-eyed fish to barter and grumbled over the handful of green coffee beans he got in exchange. The storekeeper shook his head, his expression flat. "Wartime prices, sir. I do carry a number of coffee substitutes, if you wish—parched sweet potatoes, peanuts, rye, corn . . . they all make a cup go further."

By the time Mr. Norton caught a quiet moment we'd shined up quite a few hard-to-reach spots. He glared. I stood my ground. For a long moment nobody said a word.

Finally he threw one hand in the air. "Oh, all right. I'll give you a bit to eat."

My breath blew out in a gush. "Thank you!"

He pointed to the storeroom. "Come this way. Don't let anyone see you. I can't have every street urchin bothering me. . . ."

He said some more things, but I stopped listening.

Mr. Norton found a loaf of bread with just a bit of green to

scrape off, and some carrots, and a bit of hard cheese. "Here."
He dumped them into my hands. Then he looked at the twins,
sighed, and fetched a little pail of new peas, still in the pod. "And
these too."

I doled it out even as I could. While we ate, another customer or two came in, and I listened as the young storekeeper
waited on them all, a funny mix of gruff and polite, like an
ornery old man trying to act right on Sundays. But just as we
went back into the main shop to thank him, two more women
walked in. One was plain, with dark hair, dark bonnet, dark
cape. But the other young woman had dressed all in green. Her
wheat-colored hair coiled in a simple knot, and her dress and
cape didn't have any fancy lace and such. Still, she was so beautiful it was hard not to stare.

And the storekeeper stopped acting ornery. "Good afternoon, ladies!" He smiled broadly. "Welcome to Norton's Market. How can I help you?"

"Good afternoon," the pretty one said, smiling. "We're here
from the Soldiers' Home—"

"The Soldiers' Home, ah yes, yes. You must be among the
kind ladies I have heard about, leaving your own homes to protect the welfare of your soldiers. How noble—"

"Not particularly," the woman in green said. "We do what
we can. Provide a meal, a bar of soap, a Bible. Write letters
home for those who can't. I'm Miss Lynne, and this is Mrs.
McAllister."

"Some of our supplies haven't arrived," Mrs. McAllister
said. "We hope you can provide what we need." Miss Lynne put

a list on the counter. I gawked. Even her gloves were green. I'd never seen the like.

"Of course!" the grocer stammered. "Certainly! I'm sure of it! That is . . . I'm most pleased to make your acquaintance. George Norton, at your humble service." Then he snapped his fingers at me. "Fetch me a coal scuttle!" Good thing he pointed, since I didn't know what a coal scuttle was. Turned out some folks need a special bucket just to shovel fireplace coals into. After that, he pointed and I fetched.

Within a few minutes he had the foodstuffs wrapped in paper and tied with string. After they did some accounting the women left, Mrs. McAllister with a big basket balanced on her hip, pretty Miss Lynne swinging the coal scuttle, which was filled with some of the smaller parcels. Mr. Norton stared after them for a few minutes.

I think he forgot about us for a spell, so I waited a bit, then presented myself. "We're grateful for the meal, Mr. Norton. Anything else we can do for you?"

"What? Oh. No." He looked around. "No, I must admit you did a fine job."

"Might you be needing this kind of help again?" I dared, but he shook his head forcefully.

"No! No. I'm sorry, I can't take you on. I manage this store for my father, but I don't own it. I can't be hiring help and giving away goods. Do you understand?"

He looked like he meant it. "Yes," I said. "And I thank you, Mr. Norton. I won't forget it. I'm going to find steady work, and when I do, I'll buy our groceries from you."

"Yes, of course." Mr. Norton nodded.

As I turned away to gather up our things, the door tinkled and a barefoot boy about Jasper's age stepped inside. He carried a dirty canvas sack under one arm. His pants were of rough stuff and too short, and his cotton shirt had a tear on one shoulder. But he was whistling.

Mr. Norton folded his arms, looking unhappy. "Nat."

The boy grinned. "I brought you some fine smokes."

"Your cigars are poorly made and overpriced."

"Yes, sir." Nat opened the sack and dumped some big cigars on the counter. "But you and I both know the soldiers and river-men hereabouts are looking for cigars they can afford. Of those, I got the best."

My eyes went narrow as I watched. When Nat had done his business with Mr. Norton, we followed him outside. "Excuse me!"

Nat turned. "Yeah?"

I took a deep breath. "Well . . . I was just wondering about your job."

"You need work?" Nat's sharp eyes quickly looked us up and down. "I might know of a job. For him, anyway." He pointed at Jasper.

"I'll take it," Jasper said right away.

Nat laughed. "It's not up to me. I work for Mr. Reubens. But I'll take you to him. This was my last stop."

"Let's go," I said quickly.

Nat took us down a street we hadn't seen, dodging through the crowds. "Usually I wouldn't do this," Nat said over his

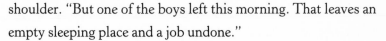

shoulder. "But one of the boys left this morning. That leaves an empty sleeping place and a job undone."

"What kind of work is it?" I asked.

"Handling tobacco. Sorting and cutting. Maybe rolling cigars. Mr. Reubens buys a few good cigars for the officers and merchants. But mostly it's cheaper to buy tobacco in bulk and roll his own."

"I can handle tobacco too!" I burst out. We'd raised a bit of tobacco on our farm. Hadn't I helped with all of it—picking and spearing and hanging and bundling? I'd never rolled a cigar before, but it couldn't be too hard.

"I don't think so," Nat said. "But it's up to Mr. Reubens."

We met Mr. Reubens inside the shabby little shop where he sold cigars and snuff and twists of plug tobacco, a mile or so away from the river. He was a man of middling size. His black hair was slicked down with oil, and when he turned his head, I saw he had parted his hair all the way from his forehead to the top of his neck like a dandy. I could tell he didn't have a woman tending him, though. That part in his hair was as crooked as a stab of lightning, and the elbows of both shirtsleeves needed patching.

When we got there a couple of skinny Yankee soldiers—they didn't look much older than Ben—were arguing with Mr. Reubens. "Your prices are too high!" one of them said, his voice squeaky as a cornered stable mouse.

"Do you see any tobacco fields outside my shop? I have to pay transportation fees. And my supply's down by two-thirds because all the farm men are off to war." Mr. Reubens didn't take his own cigar from his mouth while he talked.

I looked around while they bickered. A dusty tumble of pipe tampers and match holders and cigar holders filled one glass case. Several big stoneware jars with labels like MAKUBA and ST. VINCENT held loose pipe tobacco. A few boxes of cigars with fancy labels, each one the same size, sat in one of the cases. Rougher cigars were heaped on the shelf beside them.

"Come on, Bilby," the other boy finally said, sighing. "If you hadn't talked me into betting on that card game last night—"

"It ain't my fault! It's the army's fault for not paying us on time. . . ."

After the two soldiers left, Nat introduced us. "They're looking for work. I told them you might need a hand in the tobacco shed, since Petey left."

Mr. Reubens squinted at us, chewing on his cigar. His gaze lingered on Jasper. Then he shook his head. "I needed help this morning. I hired on a new boy this afternoon."

My heart slid down to my toes. Nat shrugged and spread his hands. "Sorry."

Back out on the street I paused. Afternoon had stretched to early evening. Jasper leaned against the wall. Mary and Maude squatted at his feet. The meal had done them good, but they were running down again. Think, Hannah. . . .

But my brain seemed too tired. Instead of thinking, I watched a couple of men arguing nearby. The tall man pounded one fist into his palm. The other man listened with hands on hips, the stump of a cigar clenched between his teeth. Then he lost his temper. He flung the cigar stub away and began talking back, a finger jabbing toward the tall man's face.

The cigar stub rolled toward us. It was the length of my pinkie finger. I stared at it like I'd never seen such before. Then I snatched it up, ground out the burning end, waved it at my brother and sisters. "See this?" I demanded. "Come back inside."

I marched back into the shop with them trailing behind like baby ducks. Mr. Reubens frowned. "I already told you—"

I slapped the cigar stub on the counter. "Look here."

"So?"

"I can get you more of these. Plenty more."

He removed his cigar from between his teeth and tapped it so ashes fell close to my fingers. "So?"

"So, I just watched two men walk out of here because they couldn't afford your cheapest cigars. Nat said you paid boys to roll your own cigars. You said you pay to wagon it in. If I find you enough cigar ends, you can take out the tobacco that's left over and mix it all together and make new cigars."

Mr. Reubens narrowed one eye. "That wouldn't make much of a cigar."

"It would make a cheap cigar. I think those soldiers would have bought some, if you'd had them."

He blew a gust of smoke into the room, his look never leaving my face. I held my breath. Mr. Reubens stuck the cigar back in his mouth, chewing furiously, both eyes gone narrow.

"Well, I'll give you a try," he said finally. "I'll pay five cents for every hundred cigar ends you bring in."

"Deal," I said quickly.

"Come back when you have a hundred ends—"

"What about a place to sleep?"

A muscle moved in Mr. Reubens's jaw. I held my breath again.

He poked his cigar at Maude and Mary. "I don't want them underfoot. I usually only keep boys."

Mary looked him in the eye. "We won't be underfoot."

"None of us will be," I said quickly. "And . . . if you give us a place, I'll mend your shirt. And take on any other sewing you've got."

His eyebrows shot skyward. He pondered a moment more, then nodded. "All right," he mumbled. "Two pennies per hundred if you want to board here too. A place to sleep and two meals a day. Nat, show them around."

Work and food and a place to sleep too! I was about ready to hug Mr. Reubens.

Nat led us through a storeroom behind the shop and out the back door. "Say, that was sharp thinking," he said.

I nodded, hoping to my bones we could find enough cigar stubs to keep our new boss satisfied.

"Mr. Reubens just ran the tobacco shop before the war," Nat told us. "Sold high-class Havanas. But once all the soldiers came, he realized most of 'em couldn't afford good cigars or pipe tobacco. So he started making his own."

A narrow alley that smelled of slops stretched behind the row of shops and warehouses. On the other side a crunch of tired-looking sheds leaned against one another.

Nat led us to one of the sheds and shoved open the door. "Mr. Reubens is renting this for the business." A strong smell of raw tobacco hung in the narrow, dim room. Two boys were unpacking leaf tobacco from a hogshead taller than either of 'em. Another sorted tobacco into piles for a boy to chop. And another was making new cigars. He sat amidst a clutter of molds, wrapper leaves, and loose tobacco, and he rolled cigars with a practiced speed that made my jaw drop.

"This is where the tobacco you collect will get turned into cigars," Nat said. "Rollers like Tom there get six cents for every hundred cigars they make. Maybe you"—he nodded at Jasper—"can move inside one day. It pays better."

I tried to take it all in. The idea of "one day" was something I didn't know how to think about.

Then Nat led us to an abandoned stable where some prosperous shopkeeper had once kept his buggy and horse. There was still some musty straw in the stalls, but the place didn't even smell of horse droppings anymore.

A couple of blankets and bundles were on the floor. "You can stay in here," Nat said. "Right now I think just a couple of the boys sleep here, so there's plenty of room. They're little kids, won't be any trouble for you. Maybe take that empty stall"—he pointed—"and hang a blanket up to make a private space."

"That'll do fine," Jasper said.

I nodded. "Where do you stay, Nat? Do you have a family?"

"Naw. But I have a little spot of my own, near the river. I like it better. Some of the fellas do that. And I think one of the boys sleeps in one of the refugee camps."

I shrugged out of my blanket roll. "What's a refugee asylum? Yesterday a Yankee officer told us we had to stay there when he thought we didn't have a place to go."

"The war's driven thousands of people into Nashville. Folks with no money and no place to go. The Yankees have taken over a couple of buildings and turned them into asylums. They give folks a place to stay, and some food, until they can figure out what to do with 'em. When there's too many refugees for the buildings, they set up camps, with tents and such. It's not for me, though. I don't need charity from the blamed Yankees."

"We don't either," I said quickly. "This is fine."

"It's dry, and handy," Nat agreed. "Of course, Mr. Reubens lets one of the boys sleep in the rooms above the shop, but I wouldn't go for that. He picks a favorite. Right now it's Tom."

Nat's voice had taken on an odd tone, but I didn't care a whit that Tom got a nicer place to stay. After spending the last night in a coil of rope, a dry stall in an old stable sounded wonderful.

We ate supper that night in the tobacco shed. A sad-faced woman who lived down the alley brought a kettle of fish stew. "Mr. Reubens won't mind feeding you tonight," Nat told us, "but you got to make up this meal before you can earn the next."

After supper we struck out to begin our job scavenging cigar ends from the streets of Nashville. By the end of the evening we had a fine total of twelve. I slumped against the wall. "This is never going to work! We'll never find enough stubs to earn any money. And now we owe Mr. Reubens for the meal."

"We'll do better tomorrow," Jasper said. "I know it."

I didn't know it, but I needed to get the twins bedded down, so there was nothing for it but to head back to Mr. Reubens's place. The light was almost gone when we pushed open the stable door. One little boy was already asleep in one of the stalls. He didn't look much older than the twins. What string of bad luck had brought him here?

We're still together, Mama.

We stretched out on our blankets. When I closed my eyes, I saw cigar ends lying in the street. That night I dreamed of Ben, picking tobacco worms with me back home, and making the chore light with his questions and talk.

CHAPTER 11

We've got to split up," Jasper said the next morning. "There's no point in four pairs of eyes looking in the same place."

I frowned. "I don't like that idea."

"We'll do better," Jasper said, stubborn as a bull calf. "I'm of a mind to head out to one of the army camps outside the city. I bet soldiers smoke a lot."

"What if something happens to you? What if you don't come back?"

Jasper snorted. "Cripes, Hannah. Nothing will happen to me. I'll meet you back here tonight." He set off down the alley without another word. I stood staring, even after he rounded the corner.

Then Mary tugged my hand. "Come on, Hannah." She sounded impatient. "We got to go to work too."

I blinked, then gently wiped a smudge from her cheek with my thumb. "You're right. How come you're so wise?" Together, the girls and I set out.

Jasper was right too. That evening, when we dumped our ends on the counter, Mr. Reubens counted a hundred and six. "Not bad," he grunted, and pushed two pennies at me. Then he reached under the counter and brought out a bundle. "And here. Mending."

Back in the stable, we crept into our stall. Jasper tied the quilt we used for privacy across the open end. "Hold these," I ordered Maude, and handed her the pennies. Then I unwrapped the bundle and found three torn shirts, a tallow candle, matches, and needle and thread.

"He's too cheap to even give you a lantern," Jasper grumbled while I rummaged for one of our tin cups. Once I got the candle lit I dripped hot grease into the cup until I could stand the candle upright.

"Let's see those pennies, Maudie," I said. Her eyes round as the coppers, she spread her fingers and held her hand close to the little pool of light.

Jasper tapped both pennies. "Look what we did."

That night I sat up and mended Mr. Reubens's clothes while the others slept in the straw beside me. When I was through I used some of his thread to make a few repairs in our own tired clothing. Then I tore a corner from my sturdy cotton apron to make a little pouch to hold our hard-earned money and stitched it inside one of the side seams of my skirt. The rest of my apron got sewn into a bag to hold cigar butts, with the apron strings providing a handy shoulder strap. My eyes were sandy by the time I lay down. *Mama, we're working hard down here so we can get back home*, I sent up silently, and tried to go to sleep.

Nine days later, twenty pennies weighed down the little purse I'd made from my apron. We so often went to bed hungry I'd reluctantly decided to buy a bit of extra food. The next day, before heading back to Mr. Reubens's for the night, the twins and I stopped at Norton's store.

"Eight cents a quart for milk!" a woman was saying as we pushed open the door. "Last week it was six! You're a vulture!"

"My good lady," Mr. Norton said forcefully, "I am nothing of the sort. The Yankee soldiers steal cows from honest folks, so there's less milk to be had. I do have some of the new tinned milk as well. But it's fifteen cents a can."

The lady went on at some length about her opinion of the Yankees and what they were doing to the good people of Tennessee. In the end she took her milk, though, before stomping out the door.

Mr. Norton snorted at her retreating back before turning to us. "And what can I do for—oh, it's you. Look, I told you before—"

"I came to buy something!" I interrupted. "We found work. I have twenty cents."

"Twenty cents?" Mr. Norton took a moment to collect himself. "And what can I get for you?"

"One penny for a spool of thread. The rest on cheese." Jasper and I had agreed on that. The widow who cooked for Mr. Reubens fed us mostly cornmeal or grits for breakfast, pork and hominy or beans for supper.

Mr. Norton pulled a red cloth away from a big wheel of

cheese on the counter, waved aside a few flies, and cut a wedge. It wasn't as big a wedge as I had hoped. But it looked good.

He counted the pennies I laid on the counter, then nodded. "You want this wrapped?"

"Please." When he handed me the parcel I tucked it carefully away in my sack. "We're going to save this for tonight, when Jasper is with us," I told the twins.

"I'm hungry now," Maude whined.

Mary looked disappointed too, but she nodded. "Fair is fair." We turned to go.

"Wait!" Mr. Norton rubbed his bushy side-whiskers with some agitation. "So, you really saved up your pennies and brought them back here to spend?"

"I told you I would. We don't make a lot of money, but when I can, I'll shop here."

He stroked his whiskers a moment longer, then smacked his hand on the counter. "If you dust my shelves again, I'll throw in a little extra food. Deal?"

"Deal!" I said quickly. Dusting for Mr. Norton would take some time from our other work. But having extra food to surprise Jasper with was worth it.

I dusted the merchandise carefully, from the little papers of seeds in an open wooden box to the rakes and shovels hanging on the back wall. In the midst of it all the two ladies from the Soldiers' Home came in. I recognized Miss Lynne first. She was dressed all in green again and hummed a sweet tune as she looked over the goods. I didn't realize I was staring until she smiled at me. "Is something wrong, child?"

"No, ma'am," I said quickly, feeling Mr. Norton's frown like a cow prod. "I just never saw so much green. But it sure is pretty."

Her sweet laugh could have chased away a storm cloud. "Green is my favorite color. It makes me feel like springtime. And the soldiers seem to like it. Being cheerful for them is part of my work."

"They must be much heartened, then," Mr. Norton said. I edged away, but not before I saw him, when the older lady had turned away, let his hand rest on hers for a moment. She didn't seem to mind, although her cheeks got pink as azalea blossoms.

When Miss Lynne and her friend had left, and I finished my dusting, Mr. Norton rewarded me with a handful of flyspecked dried apples and a few leaves of new lettuce. "Now, don't go telling anyone else," he said gruffly. "I can't have every homeless child in the city hanging about. You hear?"

"I hear." I gave him a cheerful wave as we headed for the door.

We might be living in a stable, but I concluded not to live like animals. The boys used a stinking privy in the alley behind Mr. Reubens's shop, but the door didn't latch, so I lugged home a broken crock I found in an alley to use as a chamber pot. I gave Mr. Norton a penny for a slice of lye soap the size of my thumb, and that night borrowed a tin basin from the shop after work, and sent Jasper to fill it up at the pump down the lane. "And be careful hauling it back," I ordered, "or you'll slop half out."

"It takes forever to prime that stupid pump," Jasper grumbled.

"Go," I said, and when he brought it back I picked out the tangles and washed the little ones' hair, and mine too.

"Put it in a braid," Mary instructed, as if I might have forgotten.

"Quit pulling!" Maude complained, and for a moment I almost felt like normal.

Jasper got a ragged haircut with a pair of twine cutters also borrowed from the tobacco shed. "Ow!" he yelped, twisting like I'd branded him.

"Oh, hush." Then I made him get another clean basin full so we could wash the rest of us too.

Every morning Jasper hiked out to the army camps. Maude and Mary and I stayed in the city.

Nashville sprawled over six square miles, and all kind of folks lived there. Most of 'em were women, of course, since so many men were off fighting. Some were Rebels to the bone, and they stood in clumps and looked sour whenever troops marched past. Some didn't mind walking with their gloved fingers tucked in Union officers' arms, or riding in carriages with them. Too many crept through the streets in black dresses and veils.

Nashville had a big public square by the City Hall and Market House, with offices at one end and hundreds of covered stalls for merchants and farmers at the other, and it was always busy. That made for good picking. Yards around some of the empty warehouses and homes where soldiers stayed were good too.

My favorite spot was Miss Lynne's Soldiers' Home in the

old three-storied Planters Hotel at the corner of Summer and Deaderick streets. The first time we wandered by I heard a glory coming from one of the windows near the back.

"A piano, most likely," Mr. Norton guessed later, when I stole a quiet moment and tried to describe the sound. "Or maybe a pianoforte."

Whatever it was, it was something to hear. Even with the windows closed I could hear the music, and one of those aid ladies singing for the hurt soldiers. Sometimes men joined in too, hurt soldiers or doctors maybe. I'd wander up and down the back alley, trying to look like we belonged, until Maude or Mary got impatient and dragged me back to work.

The Soldiers' Home was good for that too. In fair weather soldiers lingered in front of the Home or on one of the balconies, and some of them smoked—although the ladies scolded them for it. Once I saw Miss Lynne approach a man. She didn't look too fierce, but the man threw away a new cigar he hadn't even lit yet. Mary snatched it, and Mr. Reubens counted it as ten ends.

The best ground was along the Cumberland. Just about any day ten or more steamships tucked into the bank where sweating men lugged off huge piles of hay, corn, pork, beans, bread—all kinds of supplies. Teamsters wrestled their wagons back and forth all day long, hauling loads to army warehouses. With all the traffic, the mule drivers and merchants and steamship passengers, it was good picking.

The twins, bless their hearts, did their share. Maude mostly clung to my skirt. After she saw those two pennies, though, she sometimes broke away to snatch up a stub.

Mary learned a new trick. One day we spotted a man wearing what they call a stovepipe hat, smoking a cigar and barking orders at some of the haulers. When the cigar was down to almost nothing he tamped it out on a hogshead barrel but didn't fling it aside. We watched for a moment, then I jerked my head at the girls. Time to go. If we lingered too long in one place the clerks, and sometimes policemen, chased us off.

But Mary pulled away and marched up to him. I saw her lips move, and she pointed to the stub. He handed it to her, and she trotted back to me. "Here, Hannah." She dropped it in our sack.

"Mary! What did you say to him?"

"I just asked him for the stub." She looked confused. "Did I do wrong?"

I had to shape words around the lump of pride and sadness balling in my throat. "No, Mary. You did just fine." I didn't watch where I was going as I turned away—

"Watch it!" someone yelled.

I jumped from the path of a heavy handcart filled with coal. "I'm sorry," I started to say to the young man straining under the handles. Then the words died in my throat.

Ben.

I grabbed my elbows, hunched up like I was cold. He let the cart rest. I looked at the ground, then felt pulled to study his face. I tried to get past him throwing stones at us, and turning his back the day we'd lost Star. I looked for the boy who sang "The Ploughboy" while fighting down a furrow and laughed to see baby flickers squawking for their breakfast. There was a set to his jaw I hadn't known before. Hollows beneath his cheekbones.

A hard look in his eyes. But he was of Cumberland Mountain.

For a long moment I couldn't wrap my tongue around a word. Finally a question popped out: "Where's Sary?"

"She's at the camp. We're staying at the refugee camp in Edgefield. She stays there during the day while I'm working. It's not safe for her down here."

My face grew hot. Maude and Mary were a good piece younger than Sary! "Well, we're not staying at any old refugee camp," I snapped. "I wouldn't take charity. Camerons tend their own. We're *working* for our room and board, all four of us."

Ben's eyes darkened. He grabbed the handles of his cart and stomped toward one of the steamboats.

Tears stung my eyes. "Come on, girls, let's go. *Let's go!*" I hurried toward the quiet end of merchants' row, where we'd spent our first night in Nashville. I wanted to kick something but couldn't find a likely choice. Same with punching. Finally I snatched up a stone and heaved it into the Cumberland, hard as I could.

My heart felt as heavy and cold as that stone.

"Let's go," I said again, more tired than angry now. Soon we were climbing the hill to that glory building I'd thought looked fit for heavenly angels, our fine new state capitol. Troops were camped in the muddy yard, and we sometimes made the climb to pick tobacco near their tents. Today I just wanted to look toward the eastern hills.

"See out there?" I asked, pointing. "Somewhere, way in the distance—that's home."

Mary and Maude sat in the grass and soon were playing with

acorns, and talking in their language. I stared east. What had happened at our farm? Had someone finished hilling the potatoes, or were they bursting green toward the sun? Had someone harvested the cabbage, or had the heads split and fallen? Was that last crock of Mama's stewed raspberries still sitting in the springhouse, or had someone taken it?

"We'll go back to Cumberland Mountain," I muttered, hands clenched into fists. "Just you wait and see."

ummer faded slowly, and with it the yellow days. We heard the Federal Army had occupied Knoxville, but the Confederates were trying to take it back, and I wondered what new ugliness was being visited on the mountain folks. Late September brought a week of rain before a cool dry spell. One fine day a farmer gave us a pumpkin that had fallen from his wagon and cracked. We roasted it over a little fire we built behind the stable and gobbled it, seeds and all.

"Do you suppose our pumpkin vines at home bore good fruit?" I wondered wistfully, licking my fingers.

Jasper's eyes got a faraway look. "Likely they did. And do you figure the grapes are turning ripe on the ridge behind our place?" He sounded needy, and I was glad of it.

In October the maples on the hills around Nashville turned yellow and red. I imagined the ridges of Cumberland Mountain doing the same. "I wonder if the neighbors harvested the corn," I mentioned to Jasper. "Or did it get left to the deer, do you suppose? Do you think the hickory trees over the ridge dropped a good harvest? And I wonder if any of our neighbors have a hog left to butcher?"

Jasper shrugged. "It don't much matter to us now, does it?"

I blinked. "Most certain it does! By next year this time, we'll be back picking our own corn."

In November I dreamed of wild turkeys gobbling among the doghobble thickets on Tucker Knob, and fried pork served up with crackling bread crumbled in buttermilk. Mr. Norton surprised me with the gift of two stringy turkey legs left, he said, from his dinner. "This tastes as good as Mama's fried pork served up with crackling bread and buttermilk," I said while the four of us sat in our stall gnawing away. "Remember hearing wild turkeys gobble up in the doghobble thickets on Tucker Knob?"

"Hannah, Maude took more than her share," Jasper whined.

"I did not!" Maude shot back while Mary said, "She did not!"

"Stop fussing, all of you!" I snapped. "I was talking about home!"

"When do you think we'll have enough money to go home?" Mary asked.

"I don't know," I began, like I always did.

Jasper shook his head. "We'll never have enough."

I glared at him. "Jasper! We will too!"

"You keep promising things are going to be like they were before the war. Ain't never going to be, Hannah."

"I got us here, didn't I? And found us work when we needed it?" I demanded, and Jasper had to allow that yes, I had done those things. "So there, then."

He shrugged. I stomped outside and took a quick turn around the alley to settle down.

Maude and Mary were asleep when I got back. I stared down at them, seeing every tear in their bedraggled dresses. Mary's cheeks looked sunken. Maude had one arm around Dolly and her tin cup in one hand. I watched their chests rise and fall.

Jasper jerked his head, and I crawled by him. "Look," he muttered in a low tone. "I'm not trying to sound hard. Picking tobacco earns us enough pennies to stop by Mr. Norton's every week or so for some extra food. And I know you got a bit extra saved toward some new britches for me."

I nodded. I couldn't patch his pants with pieces of my petticoat, like I did to the shoulders and elbows of my own dress.

Jasper took a deep breath. "But . . . you think we can save enough to buy a mule and cart and supplies? Not likely."

I felt tears prick my eyes. "How can you give up? We can work harder—"

"Hannah! You got to face up to what's what."

I leaned my head against the stall wall. Neither of us was afraid of hard work. Picking tobacco ends from the streets was dirty work, done from first light 'til last every day—even the Sabbath—but at the farm we had worked just as hard. There had been no tomorrows for me in the mountains beyond more of the same.

But those tomorrows had been *mine*. I'd never thought of having any life beyond scrabbling in rocky fields beside some cabin in the blue and green mountains, trying to coax enough corn and sweet potatoes from the stubborn ground to provide for

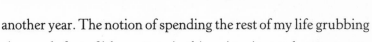

another year. The notion of spending the rest of my life grubbing cigar ends from filthy gutters in this noisy city made me want to crawl under the straw and never come out.

"I wanted to sing in a choir," I whispered. "Just on Sundays, then go home to my own place." *I dream of Cumberland Mountain,* Ben had said. . . . I remembered telling him I wouldn't be his friend anymore, so certain-sure I knew right from wrong. I remembered the look in Ben's eyes when I said it.

"Jasper . . . did you ever say something, or do something, then wish you hadn't? Wished it so bad it was like a chewing in your gut?"

"What are you talking about?"

I sighed. "Do you suppose Pa ever wished he'd stayed home? Do you think he ever lay awake at night in some far-off army camp sick with the knowing that he'd made a mistake?"

"Hannah, he—no!" Jasper muttered. He lay down on his quilt and rolled away from me.

"I'm sorry," I whispered, touching his shoulder, before lying down beside him. I shouldn't make Jasper's memories clarty as mine.

Two cats yowled from somewhere down the alley. Maude and Mary were sleeping peacefully. "Jasper," I whispered a few moments later, "did you ever figure out what urged Pa to leave us in the first place?" I waited but heard only a mouse rustling in the straw and my sisters' and brother's deep, even breathing in answer.

"Without understanding that," I went on, still whispering, "I don't know how to deep-down forgive him for going off.

But . . . I do understand now what it feels like to carry the weight for a family. Sometimes the right way isn't as clear as a body might think."

December brought a blast of icy weather. Wind blew through the stable walls at night, and we slept curled together like puppies. And Mr. Reubens's tobacco sorter disappeared—just up and didn't come to work one day.

Jasper got moved into the tobacco shed to take his place, sometimes sorting the tobacco Mr. Reubens bought from farmers and sometimes pulling apart the cigar ends we brought in and dividing that by grade—high and low. We earned a few extra pennies because of it. Most days we had split up anyway, and gone hunting for ends in different places. And the money was surely welcome. But there was something about the change that gnawed at me.

"Mr. Reubens told me today I'm doing a good job," Jasper said one evening while we got ready for bed. "He said he might teach me how to roll soon."

Rolling cigars paid better yet. But Jasper didn't sound happy. "What's wrong?"

Jasper glanced at Mary and Maude, already curled on their quilt, playing with Dolly. "Smelling that tobacco all day makes my head ache. If I don't save a bite from breakfast to eat around noon, I get sick to my stomach."

"Oh, Jasper . . ."

"And it doesn't seem right that I'm working inside while you three are out in the cold all day."

"I guess." I was ashamed to let on that I'd already thought about it. I had Mama's cloak, and thick woolen shawls for Maude and Mary. But the cold still knifed through.

Jasper crumbled an old piece of straw. "I asked Mr. Reubens if you two could work inside too, but he said no. He reminded me he doesn't usually hire girls at all. I figured I better not say any more."

I put a hand on his arm. "You did right, Jasper."

"There's something else. Did you see Tom tonight?"

Tom was the cigar roller, Reubens's favorite, who got to sleep in the spare room over the tobacco shop. I tried to think back to the evening meal. "Not to notice, I guess."

"He kept to the corner. Hannah, he came in this morning with a big bruise on his face. Minded me of the time those bush-whackers beat Mama."

That memory shivered down my backbone. "Maybe he fell."

"It didn't look that way to me. I asked, but he said it was no concern of mine."

"It isn't, I guess." Everyone was clawing their own way in the world, I figured, and had stories that didn't need telling.

"I guess." Jasper didn't sound convinced.

The next morning at breakfast I slipped a glance at Tom. He slouched in the corner again but lifted his head when the cook came past with a bowl of grits. His eye was swollen purple, and an angry bruise showed on his cheek. Jasper was right. Something uneasy slithered into my belly.

The girls and I ate quickly, said good-bye to Jasper, and

headed out to the alley. Nat was standing by the door and caught my eye. "Hannah."

"Yes?"

He spun his cigar sack, back and forth, back and forth. I waited, more unease coiling inside. "Listen," he said finally. "I just wanted to tell you . . . keep an eye on Jasper."

"What do you mean?"

"I mean trouble is coming. I've seen it before. Tom's not going to be here much longer."

"What do you mean?" I demanded again. "What's that to do with Jasper?"

He shifted from one foot to the other, glancing toward the back of Mr. Reubens's shop. "Just tell him to be careful." Then Nat hurried away.

The girls looked at me with worried eyes. "Is Jasper in trouble?" Maude asked.

"Wait a minute." I poked my head back in the tobacco shed. Tom was at work with his molds and leaves and shredded tobacco. Jasper was already hunched over the corner table, pulling apart cigar ends and sorting the tobacco inside. He didn't notice me.

I chewed my lip, then shut the door again. I'd tell him what Nat had said later. Tom's trouble had nothing to do with Jasper. "Jasper's all right," I said, knotting Mary's shawl more tightly. "Let's go to work."

We had a good morning by the river. Then we headed for the Soldiers' Home. Something about that day gave me a hunger to see Miss Lynne in all her green, and to wander nice and slow past that back-parlor window where the piano was. But I didn't see Miss Lynne, and no music squeezed out to the street, and I couldn't quite shove Nat's warning out of my head. Nat was a sturdy sort. Not one to cluck about nothing. I wished I'd talked to Jasper after all.

Mary and Maude were sharp as ever, snatching up stubs from the gutters and walkways. Then we spotted three Union soldiers walking slowly down the street toward the Home. A stout one was smoking a cigar. They stopped beside the building, talking. I figured they had paused to let the stout man finish his cigar before going inside.

I started looking through my bag like I'd lost something, careful not to catch anyone's eye, trying to look like I belonged there. Mary wandered up to the men. "Excuse me, sir," she said, sweet as molasses. "Can I have the end of your cigar?"

"What's that?" The stout man didn't show any sign of giving it up.

But one of the other men squatted beside Mary. "And what do you want his cigar for, little girl?" He had hair and a beard the color of combed flax, and blue eyes that crinkled around the corners.

I edged closer. Mary had asked a hundred men the same thing, and gotten her end or not, but no one had ever taken much interest. "We get pennies for them," she said finally. "Two pennies for a hundred."

He stroked Mary's hair. "That sounds like a hard way to earn money."

"Good heavens, Stratton, don't touch her." The stout man sniffed. "She's filthy."

Bristling like a porcupine, I grabbed her hand. "She's my sister," I said. "Come on, girls, let's go."

Stratton straightened up. "I didn't mean to frighten you," he said. He seemed nice enough. But then, so had Jack, before he stole our mule.

"You didn't. But we've got work to do."

"Wait," Stratton said. He rummaged in his pocket. "I don't smoke, but . . . oh drat, I don't have . . . here. Will this help? I'm afraid I'm not carrying much." And he dropped some pennies into my hand.

I stared, counting quickly. *Twelve pennies* . . . the same as *six hundred* ends!

"You'd be doing me a favor," Stratton said quickly. "I hate having loose change clang in my pocket. Please, take it."

"Well . . . thank you," I said finally. "I won't waste it, I promise."

"Where are your parents?" he asked quietly.

Maudie spotted an end on the ground and darted to grab it. "They're dead," Mary told him.

"I'm sorry." He shook his head, then looked at me. "Listen. I'm a doctor. One of the places I look after is the refugee asylum at the Shelby Medical College. There are lots of women and children there. It's not a perfect place. But it's better than this." He nodded at Maude as she stuffed her latest prize into my sack.

Steam rose up inside. "We do all right. We don't need charity."

"I didn't mean—" Dr. Stratton began, then his eyes went wide. "Watch out!"

I whipped my head around as a pile of kegs tumbled from an overloaded dray—toward Maude, crouching in the street. My bones went cold.

"*Maude!*" Mary screamed.

Maude looked up, scrambled, fell. One of the kegs burst against a hitching post. Two-penny nails splashed over the curb.

We were beside Maude by then. She was crying, and I heard some of the soldiers bellowing at the drayman for being so careless. "Maudie, are you all right?" I reached to pick her up. Mary clutched her hand.

"Don't move her!" Dr. Stratton ordered. "There, there, you're safe now," he said gently to Maude, all the while feeling her arms, her legs. "Can you move your head? Your toes? Does anything hurt?"

I felt frozen inside. Frozen solid.

"She's fine." The doctor eased her up, and I pulled her close. "Just frightened."

I couldn't answer. I shut my eyes and squeezed Maudie tight, and wrapped my other arm around Mary. They felt so fragile. I felt Maude's sobs quiet, felt my own pounding heart begin to quiet too.

Finally I opened my eyes. The drayman was still arguing with one of the soldiers. The stout man stood over the four of us. "Dr. Stratton? They're asking for you inside, if this little drama is over."

"Go on," the doctor barked. "I'll be in shortly." Then he looked at me. "What's your name?"

"Hannah Cameron," I said reluctantly.

He stared me straight in the eye. "Listen to me, Hannah. You can't let this happen again. You need to get these children off the streets. If you'll bring them—"

"No!" I yelled, shoving to my feet. I almost stumbled—Maudie was heavy—but I didn't let go as I turned away. "I can take care of her. I always have. I always will!"

"Think about it!" he called after me. "You can change your mind. Come to the Shelby Medical College at Broad and Vine. Ask for Dr. Stratton!"

His words just made me hurry all the faster. Tears burned my eyes. He thought I wasn't fit. As for that nasty stout man—

"Hannah, put me down!" Maude gasped, squirming. "You're squeezing me."

I planted her for a good look-over. "You're truly all right?"

"Truly." She nodded. "I'm sorry, Hannah." She peered at me anxiously.

A boulder seemed to be pressing my chest. "It's not your fault. It's mine. I should have been paying attention."

We walked the rest of the way back to Mr. Reubens's in silence. I'd never quit so early in the day before, but I just didn't have it in me to go any longer. Then I realized that in the commotion I'd dropped the money Dr. Stratton had given me.

I felt dizzy and leaned over for a moment, hands on knees. *Twelve pennies.* Twelve pennies, no doubt already grabbed by eager hands.

"Hannah?" Maude asked.

"I'm all right." I straightened and tried to smile. But as we headed on, I saw us as that doctor had: dirty, skinny, picking up the trash even mule drivers threw away as useless.

But what choice did we have? Go to the refugee asylum, become dependent on Yankee soldiers who were sometimes nice, sometimes mean, and could be gone tomorrow? Camerons tended their own.

Besides, hadn't I told Ben that I'd never sink to such?

I'll talk it over with Jasper, I thought wearily as we turned in the alley behind Mr. Reubens's tobacco shop. My brother was growing a good head on his shoulders.

I walked to the tobacco shed straightaway. But then I stopped cold. A couple of the little boys were at work, but there was no sign of Tom—or of Jasper.

"Where's Jasper?" Mary asked anxiously.

"I don't know. He and Tom can't both be at the privy at once." I struggled to keep my voice even. In all the trouble at the Soldiers' Home, I'd forgotten what Nat had said that morning. Now his words pounded in my ears.

We checked the stable—empty. I ran across the alley to the tobacco shop. The back door was ajar, and I followed the sound of voices through the little storeroom to the shop. Mr. Reubens sat on a stool behind one of the counters. Jasper perched on another, looking like something he'd eaten wasn't setting too well. I walked through the door just as Mr. Reubens put one hand on Jasper's knee.

Jasper jumped up—because of the hand or because we came in, I wasn't sure. "Hannah! What are you doing here?"

"What are *you* doing here?"

"I invited your brother inside for a business discussion," Mr. Reubens said calmly.

"What kind of discussion?" I looked from Mr. Reubens to Jasper and back again.

Mr. Reubens tapped tobacco-stained fingertips together. "Tom has left my employ. I've decided to promote Jasper to roller. I'm pleased with his work."

"Well, that's good," I said slowly. I felt like I was walking down a creek bed, feeling my way while the rocks shifted and rolled beneath my feet.

Reubens smoothed a hand over his oiled hair. "As part of the promotion, I've invited Jasper to move his things into the spare room upstairs."

I looked at Jasper. He caught my eye, then stared at the ground. "No," I said. "We'll stay where we are, all of us."

Mr. Reubens cocked his head. "I think that should be up to Jasper—"

"I said no." I made my voice firm. "We'll stay together in the stable."

"That is no longer an option—" Mr. Reubens began. Just then two big men in workmen's clothing pushed open the door. One was after cigars, the other a pouch of pipe tobacco.

While Mr. Reubens waited on them I jerked Jasper to a back corner. "Jasper, what is this all about?"

"I don't know." He looked miserable as a cornered rabbit. "But Hannah, he said if I worked hard, he'd buy me a new set of clothes, and you girls too. We need to think how to best take care of them." He jerked his head toward the twins. "Maybe—"

"No. No!"

The customers stopped talking. Mr. Reubens turned his head and gave me a look that shivered my knees.

I grabbed Jasper's arm and pulled him through the storeroom, with the girls trailing close enough to step on my heels. On out the back door. Across the alley.

"Hannah, what are you doing?" Jasper demanded. He finally wrenched free as I tugged them into the stable.

"We're leaving." I jerked down the quilt over our stall door and surveyed the little home we'd made: four sleeping spaces in the straw, our tiny cache of belongings stored neatly in the manger. I started making up a bedroll, then noticed Jasper standing still, chewing his lip. "Don't you want to go?"

"I don't know what to do," he admitted. "Mr. Reubens's never done a mean thing to me."

"Did he hit Tom?" I demanded.

"I don't know for sure."

"Well, *I* know for sure." Somehow, I did know. "Jasper, I just don't trust him."

"I don't either," Jasper admitted. "And I didn't like the idea of us being separated. But—"

"I hate that most of all." I jerked the string on one of the quilt rolls like it had done me wrong.

In no more time than it takes a chicken to drop an egg we

were packed and ready, our lumpy blanket rolls over our shoulders. I nodded to the twins. "Come on, girls—"

A shadow fell across the door: Mr. Reubens. Jasper took a step closer to me.

"Well," Mr. Reubens said after a moment. "I see you're turning down my offer, Jasper."

"Yes, sir, I am." I could tell it took an effort to keep his voice even.

"So instead, you're all going to march out into the winter with no place to go." Mr. Reubens leaned against the doorframe. All the air and light got sucked from the stable.

I struggled to pull in a good breath. "Let us pass."

He stared at us with narrowed eyes, picking at one suspender strap with his thumb. In the sudden still I heard two dogs scrapping in the alley, a baby crying in the distance, the sound of my heart thudding.

Finally, Mr. Reubens stepped aside. We scuttled outside, and I was never so glad to feel sun on my face. We walked away, and that was the last we saw of Mr. Reubens.

Jasper waited till we were around a corner before asking, "What do we do now, Hannah?"

I didn't want to answer, didn't want to have to think. I wanted to just keep marching, straight on out of Nashville. But I glanced down, and saw Maudie and Mary looking at me with those big hungry eyes. I made my feet stop marching. I had to face the day. Had I done the right thing? I didn't know. All I *did* know was that Mr. Reubens had said one truth: winter was here, and we had no place to go.

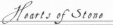

I tried to square my shoulders. "We'll find a place to spend the night, and tomorrow we'll find a new job. We found work once. We can do it again."

Mary hunkered down, as if the very notion exhausted her. Jasper looked down the street, then back at me, and I saw him remembering our first night in Nashville, spent in that coil of rope. I pictured the rivers of people we had watched flowing into Nashville all fall. A thousand people a day, Mr. Norton had told me. People like us, driven from their homes, desperate for food and shelter and work.

A woman pulled her little girl close as they walked past so she wouldn't brush against us. In the street a man trudged past, pushing a handcart and calling his wares in a high voice: "Penny pies! Penny pies! Apple, pumpkin, squash! Penny pies! Penny pies! Apple, pumpkin, squash!" That made me think of those twelve pennies. I could have bought twelve pies! The notion of sitting down to eat twelve pies made me want to laugh. I was afraid that if I started laughing, I might never stop.

To keep from it, I looked back at the others. For all the growing up they'd done, they were all waiting. Waiting for *me* to tell them what was going to happen next.

"No," I said finally. The word tasted bitter. "We're not going to look for more work, at least not right this minute." I shook my head, not wanting to voice the decision I'd made. *Ben* . . . "We're going to the refugee asylum."

very time I figured I'd reached the bottom of my valley, the path just turned a bend and went lower still. My first good look at the refugee asylum at the Shelby Medical College made me wish we'd never left Mr. Reubens's place. Tents and sheds crowded the yard, leaning against one another like windblown trees. Hollow-eyed women and children, shivering around little fires, watched silent as we walked toward the front door. I thought back to the early fall days, when we'd had a job and a place to stay and didn't have to rely on strangers' charity, and wondered why I hadn't been more grateful.

More wretched, ragged folks crammed the building, huddled on cots lining each room. I don't think there was a man among them, save a few grandfathers too old to be of much help to their families or the army. Most folks looked like they didn't have a sprig of hope left inside. They were all white. The black refugees had their own forlorn camp outside of town. I hoped like anything that the slave woman we'd met had fared well.

"Hannah, is there room for us here?" Maude whispered.

"Well . . . I'm not sure." I was half afraid we'd be turned away—and half afraid we *wouldn't* be.

Someone finally pointed us to a cramped office where two Yankee soldiers sat at a table piled high with papers and boxes. I spoke to the one with a gray beard and dark smudges under his eyes. "Excuse me, sir. Are you Captain Leghorn? A lady in the hall told me to come here."

The man rubbed his forehead. "Good God, not more. Yes, I'm Captain Leghorn. Homeless, are you?"

Jasper scowled, and I shoved my chin a wedge higher. "We do have a home. In the mountains. We just had to leave it."

"You and everyone else in East Tennessee." Captain Leghorn sighed and pulled a ledger close. "Names?"

I gave him our names, and where we were from. "And our pa served in the Union Army," I added.

"Hmph. Every woman and child who walks through this door swears ties to a Union soldier."

"Hey!" Jasper said indignantly, and pulled out the photograph of Pa in his uniform.

After barely a glance the captain scratched a few more lines in the ledger, then turned to the younger man. "Jones, is there room for them outside?"

"Actually, sir . . ." Jones leaned close to the older man and mumbled something.

"Ah. I see." He turned back to us. "Evidently two bed spaces inside have, er, become available."

"Up the stairs, first door on the right," Jones said. "You'll find it."

Those two men made me feel like we were nothing but bother. Maybe that's why I heard myself asking, "Is Dr. Stratton here? He told us to come."

"Stratton?" Captain Leghorn regarded us. "No, he's not here. He'll be making rounds in the morning."

As we trudged up the stairs Jasper asked, "Hannah, what kind of place is this?"

"A place where we can stay until we figure out what to do next."

"Charity?"

"Do you think I don't feel bad enough?" I snapped. "Can you think of something better?"

I waited. Jasper chewed his lip, finally shook his head.

"At least we're still together. At least we have a roof over our heads, and a dry place to sleep." I tried to sound like I knew just what I was doing.

The room where Jones sent us had twenty or so beds. Most were occupied by women or children, some already asleep, some staring at the ceiling or the wall, some sitting in little groups talking. A few little boys marched stick soldiers across a battle-field of patchwork. The air smelled thick with tobacco juice and the wet baby linens draped over strings to dry.

We found two empty beds in the corner, nothing but some rough planks nailed on legs. I was glad to be in the corner until I realized we were farthest from the stove. "You girls take them," Jasper said. "I'll sleep on the floor." He claimed some space with a folded blanket. I shoved the two cots together and laid out quilts and Mama's nice cloak for me and the twins.

Maude arranged our few possessions neatly under the bed. "Hannah, I don't like it here," she whispered.

"We won't be here too long," I promised but had to add, "I hope."

I noticed the woman in the next bunk watching us. She lay in bed with a wee one in her arms. That baby didn't look to be more than a few months old. "Ma'am?" I asked. "Do they give out food here?"

The woman had to get through a powerful fit of coughing before answering. "In the morning," she managed finally. "Such as it is. You done missed supper. Where you from?"

"The hill country above the Clinch River," I said. "Cumberland Mountain, near Walnut Cove. You?"

"Closer to the Holston. I think there's a few in the next room from Clinch River country," she said, then closed her eyes, like those scraps of talk had worn her out.

"There, did you hear?" I said to the others. "We'll go looking in the morning. Maybe we'll find someone from home."

We made a trip to a stinking trench out back called "the sinks," where folks were expected to make water and do their private business. Then, with nothing else to do, we tried to settle down. Maude and Mary pressed up against me. I whispered my lullabies, and before long they drifted to sleep. But hunger knotted my stomach, and the woman in the next bunk kept coughing, and her baby put up a fretful squall from time to time, and the mumbled conversations seemed loud. Our private stall at Mr. Reubens's place seemed fine, all of a sudden.

Finally I folded the scrap of tartan wool under my head and

let my thoughts wander to that long-ago time when the first of the Cameron clan left the old country, and finally made their new home in East Tennessee. They survived, I thought, pinching Mama's wedding ring hard. We can too.

In the morning a young soldier brought round a big tin pot of coffee and a basket of crackers, pale and square and tough as oak bark. "Get some coffee and soak 'em," our neighbor woman counseled. We weren't used to drinking coffee, but at least it put something in our bellies.

Dr. Stratton showed up as we finished eating. I watched while he made his way down the line, speaking to everyone, sometimes feeling a forehead or handing out pills or dosing someone with syrup from a brown bottle in his pocket. When he noticed us his eyebrows raised, and I felt my face flame. But he took his time checking the sick woman beside us. "Mrs. O'Donnell, I'm sorry your cough hasn't improved."

"I'll be well again soon," she said hoarsely. "I just want to be certain my girl is hale too." Dr. Stratton gave Mrs. O'Donnell some medicine and took a good look at her baby before moving on to us.

He sat down on the edge of our bunk. "I'm glad to see you here, Hannah Cameron. You made a good decision to come. Hello, Maude . . . or is it Mary? You'll have to remind me which is which. How nice to see you again. And is this your brother . . . ?"

I introduced Jasper. Dr. Stratton shook his hand, then asked us some questions about how we were feeling, and whether we had gotten enough to eat that morning. "You're all undernourished. Has Mary here been sick?"

"She's never been quite so hearty as Maude," I said, feeling like I'd been accused of something. "She'll flesh out some with better meals."

"We'll have to see what we can do about that, shall we?" He let his hand rest on Mary's head for a moment, looking from her to Maude. "Well, I need to get on with my inspection. I'll see you again tomorrow." He pushed to his feet.

"Dr. Stratton," I said quickly. "What are people supposed to do here?"

He looked puzzled. "Do?"

"We're used to working," Jasper explained. "We can work for our keep."

He shook his head. "No, you don't have to worry about such things anymore."

"But we want to!" I said quickly. "We don't expect charity—"

"For heaven's sake! You shouldn't have to grub for every meal. You're just children."

My blood came near to boiling. Children! I hadn't been a child since—oh, at least since Mama died, and maybe . . . maybe back since the day Ben gave me the hearthstone. At best, Jasper was half and half. Maude and Mary were children, but they'd put in many a good day of hard work. But Dr. Stratton had moved on to the far side of the room before I figured how to tell him all that.

Jasper's forehead furrowed. "We can't just sit here all day."

"Of course not. We're just eating and sleeping here while we look for work."

"All right, then." He looked relieved.

We began by searching out those folks Mrs. O'Donnell had told us about. We found several families from our county, women whose husbands were in one army or the other, and assorted passels of children. Those wise women eyed me up and talked to me like an equal. They'd all been run out or starved out. Their tales made me think we'd been smart to leave as soon as we did.

"Have you heard anything about jobs?" I asked finally.

A big-boned woman wearing a tattered straw hat shook her head. "There are thousands of people looking for work in this city."

"Wait, now," another woman mumbled. She had an empty pipe clenched between her teeth. "Those two young people—"

"Oh, yes," the first woman interrupted. "There are a couple that have found jobs. They're already gone, in fact. Come back tonight."

The four of us spent another long day tramping the streets of Nashville, knocking on doors and looking for work. My nose ran all day long. Jasper kept his hands shoved in his pockets, his shoulders hunched, the strip of skin showing between his shoes and his pants white and goose-bumped. We kept the twins hugged between us best we could. At high sun I handed three of our pennies to an old man selling hot chestnuts on a corner. I had Jasper tuck a couple in his pocket to give to Mrs. O'Donnell, who had promised to watch our things. We clutched the rest in our hands until the warmth was gone before eating them. They

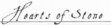

tasted of long autumn days ranging the hills with Ben, stuffing new-dropped chestnuts in burlap sacks to haul home before the squirrels and bears got 'em.

We trudged back to the refugee asylum while the lamplighter made his rounds, climbing his ladder and turning on the hissing gas lamps that lit the main streets. "Let's go see if the people with jobs are back," I suggested wearily as we climbed the stairs.

"All right." Jasper looked low.

We threaded back through the press of worn-down people to the room we'd visited that morning. A soldier was doling out the last of a kettle's worth of bean soup. "We'll be quick, so we don't miss supper in our room," I said, seeing how Jasper and the girls stared at the folks eating. "Maybe we'll hear about someone who's hiring. . . ."

Then my voice trailed away. The women we'd talked to that morning were clustered together eating their supper, their children sprawled over several bunks. But there too were the "two young people" who had been at work when we stopped by that morning. Sary McNeill perched on a bunk. Ben sat on the floor beside her, knees drawn up, scraping bean soup from a tin cup.

I stopped short and Jasper bumped into me. *"Hannah,"* he complained.

Ben looked up. His stare bored into mine, and neither of us seemed able to look away. One of the women said, "Oh, here's those new young folks from this morning." A baby was fretting. I sucked in air smelling of stale sweat and dirty diapers and onions. And I tried to pull up some sort of feeling: happiness, anger, hurt. *Something.* But nothing came, and I remembered that my heart had turned to stone.

Ben slowly pushed to his feet. "What are you doing here?" His voice was empty. I guess his heart had turned to stone too.

"We lost our jobs." I rubbed a bit of mud from one knuckle. "We came here to bide over until something else turns up." Ben nodded, and when he didn't say any more, I felt a need to fill the silence. "What are you doing here? I thought you were staying at the refugee camp in Edgefield."

"We were. We had to move here."

The big woman in the straw hat bore down on us. "So, you young folks already know each other? After all our trials, finding neighbors is a blessing."

Neighbors . . . is that what we were? Once, maybe. "We only came over because we heard you might know about work."

For a moment I thought Ben wasn't going to answer. Finally he said, "I'm still working at the docks, when they need me."

"Is anyone hiring?" Jasper sounded eager.

"No. Business is slow, this time of year. And you're too small."

Then Sary allowed, "I've been working for the army quartermaster. He hires women and girls, sometimes, to repair the soldiers' tents."

"Do you think he would hire me?" I asked quickly. Sary was just nine or ten that winter—I could sew her equal or better.

"There's a waiting list," one of the other women said. "I've been trying for weeks."

"Oh." I felt the flicker of hope die.

Ben was still looking at me. My tongue had turned to oak, but time was, we could talk without words. When I looked in his eyes, though, I saw someone I didn't know. We weren't the same Ben and Hannah we'd been before the war. I turned and walked out of the room.

We got back to our own room just as a young soldier arrived with another big kettle of bean soup. When we hurried to get our cups, I saw Mrs. O'Donnell trying to get up. "Please, ma'am, let me get your dinner for you," I said. She smiled and eased back on the hard bed. In a moment we were back with our dinner and hers too.

She pushed herself up on an elbow long enough to spoon her soup. "Thank you. I need to eat for her sake." She nodded toward her baby.

"We brought you these." Jasper handed her the roasted chestnuts.

"Oh!" Mrs. O'Donnell looked at those chestnuts like they were fine jewels, and her eyes watered up. She ate them slowly, with a church look in her eyes. "You children are kind. Were you outside all day? You were gone a long time."

"We were looking for work," Jasper said, shoveling the last of his soup.

"There doesn't seem to be any," I told Mrs. O'Donnell.

"I know who's hiring," she said.

I almost dropped my spoon. *"What?"*

"The Yankees are hiring young men to chop wood for the railroad. The Nashville and Chattanooga. He could probably get hired." She nodded at Jasper.

"I'll go down at first light!" Jasper said.

"How do you know?" I asked Mrs. O'Donnell.

"They hired my son."

"You have a son?"

"He's fourteen. We came here together. He spent a week looking for work. I wasn't strong enough to leave here." Mrs. O'Donnell had settled back on her blanket, and I had to lean close to hear. "He came back twice, after getting hired on. He said the pay was good and the soldiers were kind. Even gave him a place to stay, I guess."

"Came back twice . . ." My voice was weak as a newborn wren. "Where is he now?"

"Still working, I expect." Mrs. O'Donnell closed her eyes. "I haven't seen him in weeks."

That evening Jasper and I had a whispered argument about it, huddled together on our cot. Mary took on that stillness of hers, watching with wide eyes. Maude hugged Dolly. "I don't like it," I muttered. "Mrs. O'Donnell's son never came back! We need to stay together."

"We will stay together," Jasper came back. "I'm not going to disappear. But if the army is hiring, I'm going to take the job."

"I don't like it."

"We need the money, Hannah. We can't stay here forever."

Had I really been foolish enough once to complain that Jasper should help shoulder the burden? Well—now he was. "I just don't like it."

"I'm going in the morning." Jasper folded his arms. "Things will settle out, Hannah. You'll see."

But I didn't see that at all.

Across the way, several boys playing with a pocketful of clay marbles whooped. I felt an ache grow inside and swallowed hard. "Come here," I said, including all three in my gaze. "Let's sing before we try to sleep."

Jasper looked embarrassed. "Here?"

"We don't have to raise the rafters. How about 'The Bluebells of Scotland'?"

I leaned against the wall with an arm around each twin, and began soft and low. Jasper sat with his back to the room, head ducked. But he added the harmony line we'd practiced on our tromp west.

> *"Oh where, tell me where is your highland laddie gone?*
> *He's gone with streaming banners where noble deeds are*
> *done. . . ."*

At first I just took comfort in the old song. Then I noticed how the worry lines had smoothed from Mrs. O'Donnell's face.

> *"Oh where, tell me where did your highland laddie dwell?*
> *He dwelt in bonnie Scotland where bloom the sweet blue-*
> *bells. . . ."*

By the time we finished the last verse the noisy buzz in the room had just about died. Jasper looked ready to crawl under the bunk. Then an old woman with hair the color of snow broke the awkward silence. "Do you know 'Loch Lomond'?"

I felt a smile stretch wide. "Surely we do!"

So we sang "Loch Lomond," and "Comin' Through the Rye," and lots of others that made me think of the folks on Cumberland Mountain. Lots of folks started joining in. By the time we got to "The Camerons Are Coming" Jasper was doing a made-up jig, and Maude was skipping up and down the aisle, and just about everybody was clapping.

I clapped too, and stamped my feet, and yelled "Woohaw!" when Jasper tried a leaping turn. He fell over but came up laughing.

I slept pretty well that night after all.

CHAPTER 14

J asper left next morning before first light, headed to the rail yard near Spring Street to ask about work. Watching him go left me feeling hollow inside as an old sycamore. He stumbled back that night so tired he could hardly hold his head up.

"Oh, Jasper, look at you!" I cried. His hands, once used to ax handle and plow but softened by our months of travel and picking tobacco ends, were full of blisters—some bloody—and so stiff he could hardly bend his fingers.

"They took me on," he announced, as if I needed to hear it.

"But you're so done in. . . ." I ached inside to see it.

"How about you?"

"No luck." I pinched my lips shut tight. Jasper shrugged, looking like even that hurt, and I had a sudden memory of Pa coming in from an afternoon of stripping tobacco, his thumbs torn up raw. Mama had cupped them lightly in her hands until he smiled and said they felt better.

I took Jasper's hands in my own, light as milkweed fluff. He managed a smile too. "Don't stew, Hannah. This job pays better than I got at Reubens's. I even get a noon meal."

On the next cot, Mrs. O'Donnell stirred. "Jasper. Did you happenchance hear tell of my boy? Robert O'Donnell?"

Jasper shook his head. "I'm sorry, ma'am, I didn't meet him. But there's a lot of boys there. And they said some go out on the trains now and again."

Mrs. O'Donnell nodded and closed her eyes.

Once supper arrived, Jasper barely managed to eat his salt pork and beans before stretching out on his pallet and falling asleep. Next morning, before first light, he was up and gone again.

Dr. Stratton made his inspection visit that morning while I was combing Mary's hair after breakfast. "I have something for you two," he whispered, including both twins in his smile. "But it must be our secret. We can't have the whole place knowing you're my favorite little girls." And he slipped them each a peppermint.

"Oh!" Mary breathed, and touched hers with her tongue. Maude slipped the candy into her mouth with the look of a sinner finding salvation. A rare smile crept across her face.

I had to look away. "Thank you," I managed. "That's an uncommon treat for them."

He looked at me. "I looked for you yesterday afternoon."

"The girls and I were looking for work. Jasper got a job chopping wood at the train yard."

Dr. Stratton frowned. "I told you, you shouldn't be. . . ." He cleared his throat. "That is, I hate to think of you out in the weather all day. Especially the twins—"

"I wrap them up best I can. They do well enough," I said shortly.

He paused. "Well, anyway. I was . . . well, I was wondering if you would do me a kindness."

I couldn't imagine what kindness I could do for him! "What is it?"

"It's for my wife, actually. She's here in Nashville—"

"She is?"

"I'm fortunate. My wife was able to join me from Iowa when I was posted here. A number of the officers' wives are here. Mrs. Stratton spends many of her days helping at the Soldiers' Home. She's staying with a few of the other ladies in some rooms on College Street."

He stopped again. I waited.

"My wife has had . . . a great deal of sadness in her life. We had just one child. A daughter. Last year, soon after I joined the army and left home, our Hattie died of fever. She would have been about their age." He nodded at the twins.

"I'm truly sorry for that." I knew what loss felt like.

"My wife isn't helping at the Soldiers' Home today. Would you be willing to make a short visit to her? For so long, she could hardly bear the sight of another child. But I think . . . perhaps . . . she might take heart at meeting Mary and Maude."

I thought that through. "Well . . . we're headed out anyway. It won't hurt to stop for a while."

A big grin split Dr. Stratton's face. "Wonderful! I've made arrangements to be spared of some of my duties this morning. We can go directly."

A fierce wind was blowing that morning, but we didn't have too far to go. Mrs. Stratton's shared rooms were on the second story of a brick house. After climbing the stairs, Dr. Stratton knocked on an inner door. The woman who opened it was small and pale, wearing a dress puffed out with a hooped petticoat, and looked fragile as a hummingbird egg. She's not done much hard work in her life, I judged, but her eyes pooled so much sadness I couldn't fault her for it.

"Why, my dear!" she said when she saw her husband. Then her gaze found us in the dim hall. "But . . . who is . . ."

"These are the girls I was telling you about," Dr. Stratton said. "This is Hannah Cameron."

"Pleased to meet you, ma'am."

"And this is Mary . . . and Maude. Girls, this is my wife."

"Hello," Mary said politely. Maude hung back, clinging to my hand. For a moment Mrs. Stratton hung back too, her eyes wide, one little hand pressed against her mouth. I watched the doctor watch his wife and wondered if his idea was such a good one.

Then Mrs. Stratton stooped. "You're pretty little girls," she said softly. "I believe I can find a tin of tea inside. Would you like some nice tea?" And they nodded.

Mrs. Stratton had a teakettle ready on the little parlor stove. We all sat in the crowded room, drinking tea from thin white cups. It was even sweet! But Mrs. Stratton kept fluttering. "I wasn't expecting company," she murmured, smoothing the hair wound in a neat knot behind her neck. "Please forgive the clutter. Four ladies living in two rooms . . . we're a bit cramped."

Nothing like we are at the asylum, I thought, but I could tell

she was trying to be kind, so I didn't say it. Truth was, they were
the nicest rooms I'd ever seen.

We didn't stay long. I perched on the edge of a chair with
Maude in my lap and drank my tea while Dr. Stratton did most
of the talking. I only thought of one thing to say: "Since you
work at the Soldiers' Home, do you know Miss Lynne?"

"Why, yes." Mrs. Stratton looked at me in surprise. "Do you
know her?"

"Not really. I met her in a store. I remember her because she
dresses all in green."

Mrs. Stratton smiled. "Yes, that's Miss Lynne. She's a
breath of springtime, even in the gloom of winter."

Dr. Stratton put his teacup down. "My dear, we should be
leaving—"

"Not so soon!"

"I must attend my duties, Judith. And Hannah has other
plans for the day, I know."

I appreciated that. I stood up and reached for my cloak.

"Do you really, Hannah?" Mrs. Stratton looked at me.

"Yes, ma'am," I said firmly. "I need to find work."

"But . . . surely . . ." She looked again at her husband. "Perhaps the little girls can stay with me a while longer? They don't
need to go out again so soon? It's cruel out today!"

Dr. Stratton hesitated, looking at me. I grabbed Mary's wrist
. . . then noticed how cold it felt beneath my fingers. She hadn't
even warmed up yet.

I took a deep breath. "Would you like to stay here today
while I look for work?" I asked the twins.

Maude and Mary looked at each other, then to me. "No!" Maude whispered.

"They don't—" I began, but a howl of wind rattled the pane and swallowed my voice. I looked beyond the window, where a forlorn branch was whipping back and forth.

I crouched down and pushed some hair out of Maudie's eyes. "I need you to stay here today," I told the twins. "It's so cold out . . . it's best you stay in."

In the end I had to pull Maude's fingers from my skirt. Mary went still—she never was much for pitching fits—but Maude was weeping and calling my name as I followed the doctor out the door. My heart felt like someone had taken a flax comb to it.

On the street Dr. Stratton paused and put a hand on my arm. "You did my wife a great kindness, Hannah." His voice sounded hoarse. "Perhaps more than you can even know. God bless you for it."

"She—she's doing me a favor too, I guess. Watching the little ones and all."

He nodded. "Well, I must be off. I'm sure you can find your way." He hurried off.

I hunched my shoulders, blinking back hot tears. I felt empty as a new bee gum. For the first time in . . . in *forever*, I was all alone. Never mind that a column of soldiers was tramping past, bellowing some song about goober peas. I was alone.

I didn't, so to speak, conclude to walk down to the docks. I just found my feet moving in that direction. When I got there I leaned against a building, out of the way, my fingers tucked under my armpits for warmth. Several riverboats were moored in, but there wasn't as much traffic as there used to be. It only took a few moments to spot Ben, manhandling a heavy cart of coal. His arms had muscled up something powerful. The rest of him looked like a forked stick with ragged britches on.

The wind tried to shove me aside, but I might have stood there all day if he hadn't happened to glance my way. He didn't stop, but on his next pass by he looked again. After shoveling out that load, he let the cart rest by the warehouse and walked over. "What are you doing?" His breath puffed out in the cold.

"I just . . . just came to see you."

"Oh."

Ben, I wanted to say, remember that time we went down to Walnut Cove, and a boy kicked a stray hound? And how after scaring off the boy, you crouched by that old hound, scratching it behind the ears? Well, right this minute I surely feel as bad as that dog did.

Instead, I said, "How was your walk out?" Right away I wanted to grab those words back. His mother had *died* during their trek out!

His face tightened. "Hard."

"Yes." My cheeks burned. "Us too."

Ben nodded, and we both looked away. "It was heavy, being the oldest," I finally managed. "I worried about Jasper and the girls something awful."

"Me too. Once Sary got bit by a spider and she was fine, but I lay awake half the night fretting about it."

This time I nodded.

Ben looked over his shoulder. "Look, I got to get back to work."

I nodded again, and he started away. "Ben!" I called, and he turned back. My fingers found Mama's wedding ring and squeezed it hard. "Good talking to you."

He jerked his chin down and up. Then he fetched his cart and went back to work.

A short time later I presented myself at Mr. Norton's store. He almost smiled when he saw me. "Hannah! I haven't seen you in quite some time. Where are your sisters?"

"A lady is watching them," I explained. "We lost our jobs and had to go to the refugee asylum. Jasper found work at the rail yard. But I haven't been able to find any."

"I'm sorry to hear that."

"Mr. Norton, I need to work. I know you can't pay me, and I can get meals at the asylum. But I can't abide sitting idle all day. If you'll have me, I can come here and help you. Whatever needs doing."

"I don't have much work that needs to be done," Mr. Norton said slowly. "Prices are high and supplies are low." He gestured at half-empty shelves. "Business is not good."

I had a cold feeling in the pit of my stomach. I truly didn't know what I would do if he told me to leave.

Then he shook his head. "But I'd be a fool to turn away an offer like that. Yes, you can work here."

"Oh, thank you!"

"Just don't get in my way!" he barked, but I was already heading to the storeroom to look for cleaning rags.

asper left each morning before first light and headed to the rail yard near Spring Street. He spent the days chopping wood to feed the huge steam engines. For the first week or so he crawled back looking whipped. But in time his hands hardened and his shoulders filled out and he ate his supper while telling tales. "They got colored men laying down more track all the time," he told us. "The Union Army needs the railroads to keep supplies moving to their soldiers all over the South. There's a big map up on the wall, Hannah. You should see it." His eyes glowed.

I spent my days at Mr. Norton's. Sometimes Maude and Mary settled near the stove playing with Dolly or with a box of odd buttons—tin, wood, bone, gutta-percha—Mr. Norton gave them to sort. But more often than not, I took them round to Mrs. Stratton for the day.

"Why do we have to?" Maude asked, the first time we three trudged up the stairs in the boardinghouse.

"Because it's too cold for Mary to be out," I said. "Isn't Mrs. Stratton nice to you?"

"Yes," Mary said slowly.

"But she doesn't know any good songs," Maude added, and I vowed to sing that night until my voice went raw.

When I fetched them, at day's end, I found that Mrs. Stratton had washed and combed their hair, and plaited it neatly, and looped it up on their heads. My face got hot.

Mrs. Stratton watched me anxiously. "Please don't mind. It was my pleasure."

I did mind. So when Maude pulled the pins from her hair, and laid them neat as soldiers under our cot at the asylum, I didn't say a word.

"I feel like we're keeping you from your work," I told Mrs. Stratton the next time as she unwrapped the girls from their shawls.

"Oh mercy, no," she said. "I do enjoy helping at the Soldiers' Home, but . . . the other ladies do just fine without me. I love watching these little darlings."

And later, when Mrs. Stratton showed me two little capes made from brown polished cotton and lined with soft wool flannel, it was much the same. "It was no trouble," she told me, snugging one over Mary's shoulders. "This extra layer will keep the damp off. I cut up an old skirt and pettiskirt to make them. No trouble at all."

January was too harsh for even crows and Methodist preachers. We got sheets of cold rain. The city streets churned to greasy knee-deep mud, rimmed each morning with a crust of ice. Fuel was dear, and often Mr. Norton's store was almost as cold as the street. At the asylum, women and children huddled around the stoves, and very little heat found its way to our corner.

In the evenings, I helped Mrs. O'Donnell with the baby, changing her soiled linens and washing them out by the pump in the backyard. Mrs. O'Donnell's cough didn't ease, and her wee babe was sickly now too. When Dr. Stratton tended them, I saw how tight his face looked, and how his smiles didn't reach his eyes. Sometimes Mr. Norton gave me a cup of milk to bring back for them, and Mrs. O'Donnell would reach for me with a claw-like hand and say, "Thank you, child. Thank you."

Twice that month soldiers moved through the asylum, bellowing that a special train had been arranged to transport refugees north. Each time a number of families left, heading for kin or just hoping for better times in a new place. But more always took their place, strangers with the same shadows in their eyes. They came from Middle and East Tennessee, but also from Georgia, South Carolina . . . all over. The asylum was so crowded I hardly ever saw Ben and Sary. Once or twice, if we passed in the hall, we'd stop and say something about nothing until somebody felt stupid enough to end it and walk away.

Ben and Sary split up each day too. When I happened to see Ben tuck a scarf around Sary's throat one morning before they walked off in different directions, I wondered if it pained him as much as it pained me. A few days later, when we passed on the stairs, I asked him.

"I hate it." The words squeezed out.

"Me too."

And for a moment it was just like old times, each feeling what the other felt.

"Did you ever find a job?" he asked after a bit.

"Not one I get paid for. But I help out at a store. Mr. Norton—he's the one who works there—he got hurt in the war. I haul firewood inside for him, and fetch things so he doesn't have to hobble too far on his crutch, and generally make sure he has the cleanest general store in Nashville." I shrugged. "It keeps me busy."

I wanted to tell Ben about Miss Lynne, who came in 'most every day. She usually bought something. But some days she came inside and said hello with stories of "just passing by" or "needing to warm up." I could see Mr. Norton didn't mind, and I didn't either. Her smile seemed to warm the room. And just like Mrs. Stratton said, in the middle of that gray winter, Miss Lynne's green cloak and gloves and bonnet were pretty as a patch of ferns by the springhouse back home. Mr. Norton always bundled her near the stove, and she didn't seem to mind his crutch a bit. And if another customer came into the store while he was murmuring with her, he let me fetch what they needed and only came back in time to tally up the total in his ledger.

But that seemed like a lot of chatter.

"We can hear the singing from your ward in the evening," Ben said. "I heard you're right in the middle of it."

I shrugged, glancing away. "Makes me think of home, is all."

He looked like he wanted to say something, then changed his mind. He shrugged, and I nodded, and we both headed off to work.

And so we crept through January. Mary had a sick spell, full of coughs and fever, but Dr. Stratton dosed her with something, and it passed. I felt like spring would never come—and if it did, that the war would go on and on, and we'd live the rest of our lives in the refugee asylum. At night, while the twins pressed against me, I let my hand dangle over the cot to feel Jasper's shoulder. It was the only way I could sleep.

The girls and I were eating breakfast one gray morning in late January when Captain Leghorn, the man in charge of the refugee asylum, stepped inside our room with the young soldier named Jones. "Attention! Attention, please." He waited until the room was silent. "Two steamboats have been made available for the transportation of refugees to points north. Everyone is to gather their belongings and proceed to the front yard, where you will be escorted to the river. Wagon transport will be provided for anyone too sick to walk."

A surprised murmur rose. Some of the women didn't move. Others began gathering children, reaching for their belongings.

"He doesn't mean us," I muttered, feeling uneasy. Captain Leghorn had announced refugee trains in the past, but he'd never said "everyone" before.

"Where are they taking us?" one woman called.

"Ohio," Captain Leghorn said. "Aid societies there will help you find work and places to live."

"But how will our husbands find us?" another woman asked, her voice rising shrill and thin.

"We're keeping records. You'll be reunited. No, no more

questions!" The captain ran a hand over his face. "Look, the army can't take care of you all here! There's too many of you, and more coming every day! This is the best we can do! Now please, pack up your belongings!" He turned to the young soldier. "Jones, see that they clear out. Keep the invalids separate." And then he was gone.

Jones's face was red, and for a moment he chewed his lip, looking for all the world like a schoolboy caught in a lie. Then he clapped his hands, walking down the aisle. "All right, now, let's get moving! Pack up, ladies. We need to get everyone packed up and outside." He stopped near our bed. "Don't just sit there."

"But we can't go!" I cried. "We—we need to stay here. We have a home in the mountains—"

"Everybody has to go."

"But my brother is at work—"

"You have to go!" he yelled, his voice shaking. And even with my skin prickling and my heart banging, some tiny part of me understood that Jones hated this too.

All around me grim-faced women were rolling quilts, tying knots in bulging bags. Even Mrs. O'Donnell pushed to her feet, her whimpering baby clutched to her shoulder. And when Jones came back and hollered at me again, my hands began to work even if my mind wouldn't, gathering our things.

Maude grabbed my hand. "Hannah, where are we going?"

"I don't know."

"But Hannah—"

"Just hush for a minute!" I fumbled with Jasper's quilts. Should I take them, or leave them? Take them.

"But what about Jasper?" Mary whimpered.

"I don't know," I managed. "I purely don't know."

A hundred women jammed the hallway, dragging bags and baskets, babies on hips, dull-eyed children in tow. Mrs. O'Donnell leaned on me. "You hang on to me good," I commanded the girls in a low voice. "No matter what, *stay right with me*. We might have to make a run for it. We're not getting on any riverboat."

In the yard I looked for Dr. Stratton, thinking he might help us, but I didn't see him. Shouting soldiers herded folks like cows. "Sick, over to the wagons! The rest of you, keep left. Left! Keep moving!" A thick line of refugees flowed from the asylum toward the street. Some squawked like dying ducks in a thunderstorm. Most plodded along with heads hung low.

Our footsteps crunched on frost. Mrs. O'Donnell stopped, a deep fit of coughing almost bending her double. "Come on, Mrs. O'Donnell," I said. "Let's get you to the wagons."

I helped her to the street, where another soldier was hollering. "Sick only here! We don't have space for everyone." He pointed at me. "You have to walk."

"I will," I snapped. "But this woman is sick. I'm helping her."

He looked at Mrs. O'Donnell and nodded, even offered his arm to help her.

Mrs. O'Donnell pressed my hand. "Thank you, Hannah. You've been a blessing."

I watched as the soldier struggled to get her on the mounting block. "Maude and Mary, hold hands and stay right here," I ordered. *"Don't move."*

I helped Mrs. O'Donnell into the wagon. The back was filled with straw, and I eased her down. "Thank you," she murmured. "We'll manage now."

"But Mrs. O'Donnell, what about your son?" I couldn't help asking. "How will you find him?"

"I don't know," she whispered. A gust of wind caught the ragged blanket wrapped around her shoulders, and her baby began to cry. "Oh—" She tried to cover the tiny girl. "If only . . ."

I began scrabbling through my quilt roll. I couldn't afford to give up much. But I did have one baby-size piece: the scrap of wool cloth from Scotland, all that was left of my mother's people.

I pressed my cheek against the wool one more time, then quickly tucked it around the baby. Mrs. O'Donnell thanked me with her eyes. I squeezed her hand before climbing down and grabbing the twins. Then more folks jostled between us, and we had to turn away.

A soldier pointed us toward that ragged line of people already flowing toward the Cumberland. Then a familiar voice, raised in anger, caught my ear.

"But why are you forcing all of us to go?" Ben McNeill stood eye to eye with a soldier no taller than he was. "My sister and I have work. We can—"

"Orders are orders!" the Yankee shouted back. "Now, get in line!"

The soldier turned away and hurried on to holler at another family for holding up the line. Ben looked around the yard, his mouth pressed in a grim line, before pulling Sary back toward the asylum. People were still trudging out the door, and for a moment I lost view of them. Then I saw Ben and Sary slip around the corner of the building and out of sight.

"Come on," I muttered to the twins.

"Hey! You there!"

I looked over my shoulder and saw one of those boy-soldiers coming after us. "Back in line," he barked when he caught up. "Orders."

"We're just stopping by the sinks," I lied. "My sister has to go."

"Real bad," Mary offered earnestly.

"Well . . ."

Mary raised her voice. "*Real* bad!"

"All right, then. But make it quick." He raised his voice too, like he needed to stay in charge.

I nodded, heart thumping, and we hurried away. I had turned Mary into a liar now. I raised my chin. "Good for you," I told Mary, and she smiled.

We rounded the corner of the building and found Ben and Sary pressed against the back wall. Ben jumped, then took a deep breath. "What are you doing?"

"Same as you. Getting out of here before they ship us up the river."

He hesitated, then jerked his head toward the outbuildings behind the medical college. "Come on. If anyone yells, just keep walking."

We hurried past the stinking sinks and around a carriage house. The Yankees had established a stable yard next to the asylum, with long rows of hastily built teamsters' quarters. "Let's cut through here," Ben muttered.

The yard was busy with freight wagons, soldiers leading horses, a rider or two. I hoped we could lose ourselves in the clamor, but we hadn't gotten far before a soldier stamping past stopped to frown at us. "What are you children doing here?"

My heart was about ready to ooze out my toes. Ben stepped in front of Sary. "We're just cutting through. I thought it was a shortcut—"

The man's frown deepened. "Do you belong at the refugee asylum? You're not supposed to—"

"We're looking for cigar ends," I lied.

"What's that?"

"Cigar ends. We collect them and sell them to a tobacco shop. Usually, places where soldiers are have good pickings. We didn't mean to cause trouble."

The man nodded slowly. "I've heard of such, poor wretches—here." He rummaged in his pocket, pulled out a half-smoked cigar.

Mary reached for it. "Thank you," she said nicely. "We get two pennies for a hundred."

The man let us go. We hurried on through and came out on Demonbreun Street. "We should be safe now," Ben said. "That was good thinking."

I turned that compliment over before tucking it away in the Ben-hole beneath my ribs. "But what do we do now?" I hugged the twins tight as a blast of wind shivered through my cloak.

Ben pondered for a moment. "We have to get the girls to a

safe place. There's a refugee camp just outside town, off the Franklin Turnpike. We better head there."

"But won't they be shipping folks off too?"

"I don't think so. They usually just clean out one place at a time. Whichever is most overcrowded. If we give them made-up names, they can't track us." Ben began walking down the street.

"The doctor from the asylum—Dr. Stratton—he likes the twins. If we could find him, I think he'd help us."

"Didn't you hear?" Ben said angrily. "Those soldiers were just following orders. I wouldn't trust any Yankee soldier to keep Sary safe."

"Well, I wouldn't trust a Confederate soldier to do anything!" I flared back. For a moment we glared at each other, old wounds ripped open, our fathers' ghosts marching through our minds.

"Do what you want," Ben said. "I'm taking Sary to the refugee camp. We should be safe there for at least a couple of months."

"How do you know?"

"Because we've had to move twice before," Ben said over his shoulder.

That explained a lot. I hesitated a moment longer, then pulled Maude and Mary along after the McNeills.

he provost guards who ran the refugee camp worked in a tent. A soldier pointed us in that direction, and we found two men at work on little legless desks they held in their laps. The tent was warm and steamy. They actually had a tiny stove in there.

Ben did the talking. "We were told we could find shelter here, sir. We've been traveling a long time, and don't have any money."

One of the men frowned. "Lieutenant, didn't I hear they were cleaning out the refugee asylum at the medical college today? They'll have lots of room there. Maybe we should send these children on."

I held my breath until the lieutenant shook his head. "Sir, it's undoubtedly utter chaos there yet. We best get them set up here." He pulled his big leather-bound ledger close and picked up his pen. "Names?"

I listened to Ben give made-up names. Then it was my turn, and I didn't blink. Now, I thought, I have denied my own family name—as well as being a thief and a liar. There was a time I would have expected God or Mama to smite me for that, but I wasn't sure they paid such close attention anymore.

"You'll find room in the second row of tents, toward the end," the lieutenant said. A woman in cracked shoes and a muddy wool cape pushed into the tent, three children in tow. "We've come for such as you've got," she announced, and the men were suddenly very busy.

The refugee camp was tidier than the asylum had been. Small canvas tents stood in neat rows, back-to-back. A cookfire burned at both ends of each little street. Women and children stooped by the fires, reddened fingers fanned toward the flames.

We followed the lieutenant's directions and found two empty tents, side by side. Ben and Sary claimed one, and the twins and I the other. It was empty but for two cots, each with a thin straw mattress. The front and back flaps had little ties so they could be shut tight. I liked having a spot to call our own. But our tents didn't have little stoves. Our breath puffed white in the air. "You fix our things like you want them," I instructed Maude, untying our quilts. "Then wrap up and get warm, both of you."

Ben poked his head in our tent. "Hannah."

It was the first time he'd said my name in over a year. It sounded different and the same all at once. "What?"

"If you stay here with Sary, I'll go find Jasper and tell him where you are."

"Well . . . I surely don't want to take the girls out again if I can help it. I'm obliged. You and Sary were lucky to be together when it all happened. How come you weren't at work?"

"We both lost our jobs. Not enough work at the quartermaster's or the wharves this time of year." A muscle worked in his jaw. "You said Jasper was working at a rail yard, so I thought I'd see if I could get hired on too. Which one is he at?"

"Nashville and Chattanooga. And I'm still obliged." He nodded and disappeared.

I lay down with Maudie and Mary. "I'm proud of you," I whispered as they snuggled close. The smell of them, damp wool and something sweet all their own, was a comfort. I began to sing, under my breath, "The Mermaid" and then "Johnie Scot" and "The Gypsy Laddie," and soon they both relaxed in my arms and stopped shivering.

But before long the provost guard arrived, with the new refugees trailing behind. He began directing the women to tents, and I heard him speaking to Sary. I went outside and almost bumped into him.

"Who's in this tent?" he asked.

"My sisters and me—"

"That's not enough. And this girl is by herself next door. I don't have enough space for everyone. You"—he pointed at Sary—"need to move your things in here." His finger shifted toward our tent.

"But my brother needs room!" she protested, and I chimed in, "My brother will be here this evening!"

"I'm sorry, but I don't have the space!" the lieutenant said. He stamped his brogans on the ground, blowing on his fingers. "You girls need to settle in together so I can get these others situated."

Sary shot me a look like I was a hawk and her a rabbit.

"It doesn't matter, Sary," I said quietly. "We need to do what he says. We'll sort things out when Ben and Jasper get back."

She nodded and fetched her little bundle of belongings into our tent. We all curled up under our quilts and blankets. After a bit I heard Sary snuffling.

"Get up, girls," I directed. We pushed our cot over by hers, and the four of us nestled together to wait for our brothers.

The boys came back together after dark that evening. I ran my hands over Jasper's shoulders, making sure he was real. He looked glad to see us too. Sary and I explained what had happened with the tents.

"There's room for us all, I guess, if we make pallets on the ground," I said, although I wasn't sure about that.

Ben shook his head. "I got hired," he told Sary. "They said I could sleep at the train yard if I wanted. They have an empty warehouse where some of the boys stay. I said no, but I think I should."

"But . . ." Sary began. Ben gave her a look. They had a full conversation with their eyes—the way he and I used to. Then Sary nodded.

"Maybe I should too," Jasper said slowly.

"Jasper, no!" I protested. "Isn't it bad enough we're apart all day long?"

In the long silence that followed everyone stared at me. I clenched my hand into a fist, then slowly uncurled my fingers. "It's inside? This place they let the boys sleep? Warm?"

"Yes."

"Then I guess you better," I managed. "But—but will you still come back and eat with us in the evening?"

"I promise," Jasper said, and I had to settle for that.

Everyone said it was the worst winter in memory. Sometimes we had snow, sometimes not, but the cold was mean.

The provost guard made sure we had firewood and found us each an extra blanket with just a few holes. The tents were divided into groups, and the guard delivered baskets of food each morning and evening for the women to cook. Soldiers inspected the camp once a day and made sure we were bleaching the cutting boards used to chop vegetables, and covering our messes in the sinks, and a week or so after we arrived a doctor inoculated everyone against smallpox. I could tell they were doing their best for us.

But I was still miserable, so before too long I began bundling the twins up in the morning and walking to Mr. Norton's store. Sary came too. "I'm not running an orphan asylum!" Mr. Norton grumbled the first time I brought Sary along. But before we left he gave each of us a fistful of dried cherries to munch on the way back to the camp.

The four of us were walking into the city one day in early February when I heard someone calling my name. "Hannah! Hannah Cameron!"

I turned and saw Dr. Stratton running toward us. He dodged a few people and almost knocked a laundress over. "Oh, thank God. I'm so glad to see you! Where have you girls been?" He gave the twins a big hug. "I didn't know what happened to you! To any of you," he added quickly, then looked inquiringly at Sary.

"This is Sary McNeill. We were neighbors back home," I said. I nibbled my lip.

"I thought you'd been sent north!" he exclaimed, brushing hair from Maude's eyes. "My wife took ill that morning, and I was with her. When I heard what had happened I went through the records, and couldn't find a trace of you! My wife has been terribly upset!"

I traced a circle with my toe. "We ended up at the Franklin Pike refugee camp."

"But I checked the lists! I didn't see your names."

"I made up names," I admitted. "But it was mean of them to try and make us go north!"

"It seems so," Dr. Stratton agreed slowly, "but you girls can't imagine . . . the army simply can't afford to feed and shelter all of the refugees. More arrive every day. We've already had to send thousands—"

"But you won't tell on us, will you?" I demanded. I'd move on again, hide if I had to.

He touched Mary's cheek with a gloved finger. "No," he said finally. "I couldn't do that. In fact . . . I suggest instead that we visit my wife. She's been frantic, and her health has suffered because of it. Seeing you again would be a tonic." He looked at the twins. "Would you like to visit her?"

Maude and Mary exchanged glances. "All right," Maude said. *Maude* did. I opened my mouth but nothing came out.

"I'm off duty today, so I can take them over, if you're on your way to work," Dr. Stratton said to me. "You can pick them up at the end of the day. Would that suit?"

"I guess so," I said slowly. Maude and Mary each slipped one little hand into his, and I watched them walk away.

"Do you know Mrs. Stratton well?" I asked Miss Lynne that afternoon while Mr. Norton argued with a customer about the price of salt beef.

"Why, yes, I do. Why do you ask?"

"Sometimes she takes care of my little sisters."

"Mrs. Stratton is a darling." Miss Lynne pulled off her gloves and held her fingers toward the stove. "Her health is delicate, so I'm afraid her time in Nashville has been a trial. But perhaps no more so than staying in Iowa alone while her husband was here. He's devoted to her. I'm sure they take wonderful care of the girls, dear."

Mr. Norton hobbled over to join us, then balanced his crutch to take Miss Lynne's hands in his. "My dear, your fingers are like ice!" I excused myself, suddenly glad of the interruption.

Sary and I left the store a little early and walked to Mrs. Stratton's rooms on College Street. We climbed the stairs, and I was about to knock when a strange noise from behind the door stopped me. It seemed familiar, yet not. I pressed the latch and pushed open the door.

Dr. Stratton was on his hands and knees on the floor, with Maude sitting on his back. "And this is the way the general's horse rides," he was saying, pretending to buck as I stepped

inside. Mary, who was watching, clapped her hands. And Maude tipped her head back and squealed with laughter.

That was the sound I hadn't recognized. Maudie's laughter.

"Why, Hannah!" Mrs. Stratton exclaimed. She had been laughing too but stopped when she saw my face. "We didn't hear you." Maude slid to the floor, and the doctor hastily got to his feet.

"Come along, girls." I held out my hand. Maude darted over, and Mary followed.

Mrs. Stratton looked at her husband and made a little gesture. He sat on the edge of a chair so he could look me in the eye. "Hannah, we have something we'd like you to think about. My wife has offered to let Mary and Maude sleep here—"

"No!"

"—so they'd be out of the cold," he went on. "They'd be warm."

"I'm sorry I can't offer the same to you and Sary," Mrs. Stratton said. She twisted a lacy handkerchief in her fingers. "But we've had two more ladies move in with us since you were here last and . . . we simply don't have room."

They still had more room than we'd had at the asylum.

"They'd be warm," Dr. Stratton said again. "And they'll get a good breakfast in the morning."

Warm. I became aware of how warm their hands felt in my own.

"We want to come back with you," Mary whispered. Maude nodded, squeezing my fingers.

Strange thing is, that's what decided me. I knelt down and

gave them each a hug. "It's best you stay here tonight," I whispered. "But I'll be by in the morning to fetch you."

"Promise?" Maude asked.

"I *promise*."

Then I stood up and faced the Strattons. "They can stay tonight, but they're coming back to the camp with me tomorrow." It was an order.

That night got so cold that coffee froze in our tin cups almost before it was poured from the pot. Maude and Mary were safe and warm in Mrs. Stratton's rooms on College Street. Jasper was safe and warm in the warehouse at the train yard.

Still, I hardly slept. The stone in my heart seemed colder and heavier than ever before. If we were going to be separated anyway we could have stayed in the mountains, snug in our neighbors' cabins! I thought of our family Bible, rotting along the road; of sweet Star, who-knew-where; of our precious bit of tartan wool from Mama's mama, now cradling baby O'Donnell somewhere in a place called Ohio.

All gone. And all my fault.

CHAPTER 17

Febuary inched toward March. Maude and Mary stayed with the Strattons every second night. Jasper spent more time on the trains, sometimes gone for two or three days at a time. He came back telling tales of sights he'd seen and sketched rough maps in the dirt to show me where he'd been. I pretended the lines had some meaning.

"Is it safe?" I asked him one morning. "It frets me some."

"*Hannah*," he said, like I was being stupid. "All we do is haul supplies. And I don't do anything but feed the fires, and help load and unload." And he was paid for it. He brought me his wages, and I tucked them carefully into my hidden pocket, dreaming of the day we'd be able to buy a mule and cart and travel back to Cumberland Mountain.

Sary took to spending most of her time in camp. The other refugees were good women, for the most part. But they bickered about how to cook our allotment of sweet potatoes or beans, whose turn it was to fetch wash water, who rusted the tin frypan by forgetting to dry it well. Someone's tongue was always going like the clapper in a cowbell. I preferred to spend my days dusting shelves and helping customers and watching Mr. Norton whisper words that made Miss Lynne blush and smile.

But the nights stretched long.

"Sary," I said one evening, when we were alone in our tent. "Do you like to sing?"

"Well . . . I can't say I'm partial to it in particular."

"Let's try an easy one. How about 'Will Ye Go to Flanders?' You must know that one!"

Sary gave it a game try. She didn't have much of a voice, which surprised me some, given that her brother's was so strong. And I soon despaired of teaching her harmony. But as the days passed we sang now and again anyway, and sometimes some of the other refugees even joined in. We didn't have any real *sings*, like the one back at the refugee asylum. But when I heard two women singing hymns while they chopped onions, or some young'uns bellowing "Scots What Hae Wi' Wallace Bled" while they marched up and down the lane, I liked to think that I did get them going.

One night as I shivered on my cot, I heard a woman walking back and forth outside our tent, trying to settle a babe either colicky or just plain cold. The woman sang softly:

"My heart's in the Highlands, my heart is not here,
My heart's in the Highlands, a-chasing the deer;
A-chasing the wild deer, and following the roe,
My heart's in the Highlands, wherever I go.

"Farewell to the mountains, high-cover'd with snow,
Farewell to the straths and green valleys below;
Farewell to the forests and wild-hanging woods,
Farewell to the torrents and loud-pouring floods."

There was more, but she walked out of earshot. I wished Ben
had been there to hear it.

I was coming back to camp one evening, alone, when Sary ran
down the lane and grabbed my arm.

"Oh, Hannah, I've been waiting for you," she cried. "I've
been so scared—they're saying it was Nathan Bedford Forrest—"

"Wait! Slow down!" I grabbed her arms. "What did Nathan
Bedford Forrest do?" Forrest was a famous Confederate raider.
The Yankees hated him. Confederates took a fierce pride in
the man.

"He attacked a train!" she gasped. "It happened this morning. One of the provost guards said so. He said some of the Yankees on the train were killed, and others captured! Maybe some
of the laborers too!"

"What line? What train? Were Ben and Jasper on that train?"

"I don't know!"

Some of the other women pressed close. I closed my eyes,
rubbing my forehead with icy fingers, trying to think. No. Jasper
hadn't said anything about going out on a train that day. He had
to be safe. He *had* to be safe—

The women's voices pushed through. "That Forrest is a

devil," one of them muttered. Another rounded on her: "He's the bravest man that ever lived!" The politics kept treed all winter crashed down around us.

"Come along." I grabbed Sary's hand. "We'll go down to the train yard and find out."

We had to stop at the provost guard's tent first and get a special pass. The soldier on duty frowned. "Darkness is coming on. You're supposed to be in camp—"

My heart got balled up in my fist as it pounded down on his little table. "We have *got* to *find* our *brothers!*"

He gave me the pass.

The train yard was situated near Spring Street, half a mile away, and we trotted through a slushy mud. Once there I hesitated, not sure where to turn. The yard stretched in the distance, a fearful tangle of tracks and engines and strings of train cars. I saw a few soldiers, more laborers. There was rubble lying about, and huge piles of wood—some chopped, some not.

"Is Jasper Cameron about?" I asked some boys, and when they shook their heads, I turned to a Yankee soldier. "Sir? Can you tell me about the raid?" But the man shook his head too, and hurried by.

I asked everyone in sight and was fighting real panic when I heard my name. "Jasper!" I cried, and ran to give him a big hug. "Thank the Lord!"

He jerked away. "Hannah, don't!" He flushed red, quickly looking around to see who might have seen. "What are you doing here?"

"We heard about the raid! I was scared!"

He scoffed, waving his hand. "You should have waited in camp. I'm safe."

"I didn't know that!"

"It wasn't even my line! It happened on the Nashville and Northwestern!"

"Well, I didn't know that either!"

"You're treating me like a child!"

"You are a child!" At least I wished he was. How I missed the days when he leaned on me! Why had I found that burden so heavy?

We might have gone on hollering at each other if Sary hadn't interrupted us. "Jasper, where's Ben?"

Jasper led us to a barn-size woodshed where Ben was stacking split wood into a huge pile. We had to explain everything all over again. "I hadn't even heard about the raid," he said. But at least he didn't argue with Sary about it.

By the time we all trooped back to the camp, I was too tired to bicker with Jasper anymore. We ate our meal in silence, and the boys trudged back to the rail yard for the night.

"Hannah," Mr. Norton began one morning, on what Mama used to call a dark and drublie day. A cold rain was beating down, flowing across the big front windows, turning the street outside into a sea of mud. We hadn't had a customer in over an hour, and I'd already tidied the store shelves. Mr. Norton had even given up his usual perch behind the counter and settled stiffly in one of the chairs beside the stove. "Come put the kettle on, there's a good girl. I took a basket of sassafras roots in trade for a bar of soap yesterday. A bad trade on my part, I'm sure—why, what is the matter?"

Tears spilled down my cheeks. I felt foolish as a turkey in the rain, and swiped them away. "It's the sassafras," I quavered, then had to stop. Mama had gathered tender sassafras roots every spring to make tea, and depended on it to ward away the winter chills and keep a body in good order. The last time I tasted sassafras tea was the day we buried her.

"Sit down," Mr. Norton ordered, and *he* put the kettle on and brewed up a fair pot of tea. We sipped for a few minutes. The rain changed to sleet. "Now. What's the matter?"

"I miss my mother," I heard myself saying. "And my pa too, I guess. Even though . . ."

"Even though . . . ?"

"Even though I'll never understand why my pa went to war. I've tried six ways from Sunday to figure that through and still don't know."

The storekeeper stared at the stove. "That I couldn't say."

"I used to ask some of the men why they went, back when we were picking cigar ends by the hospitals." I remembered hearing a different reason from every man:

"Well," one had said, "we had a speech and a parade and I ended up at the enlistment tent."

"I believe in the Union," said another.

"I was sweet on this little gal, and she shamed me into it."

"The country needed me."

"It seemed like a lark. Me and my brothers, we all enlisted."

"I had joost come here, to America, ya? And I say, this country, she give me a home. So I will fight for her."

"Slavery is an evil that must be purged away."

"I don't even remember anymore." This last had come from a man who'd been blinded, but I could tell by the quiver in his hands, the haunt in his tone, that he still saw plenty of pictures in his head.

I told Mr. Norton, "None of that seemed to make sense for Pa to go to war." I listened to a mouse scrabbling hopefully in the back room. "Mr. Norton . . . why did *you* join up with the Confederacy?"

He was silent for a long time. Then, "I was a boy, with a boy's heart. It seems like a long, long time ago. I'm not the same person now."

That wasn't much of an answer.

"It's just been so hard," I finally mumbled. "I thought coming to Nashville would keep the family together."

Mr. Norton hitched his chair closer to the stove. "Family is worth holding on to."

"Well, I'm losing mine. Jasper likes his work on the railroad. And Maude and Mary . . . the Strattons take good care of them. Give them food, and keep them warm. They even found new shoes for them."

"Ah. I see."

"I've already lost my friends. Soon I won't have a whisper left of anybody." I managed a watery smile. "Except you, Mr. Norton. You're the only friend I've got."

"Oh, don't be a goose," he said. But he reached over to pour me more tea.

I took a sip, thinking about how I always thought about losing my family and losing Ben in the same breath. I remembered Mama telling Mrs. McNeill that we'd be her family, the day her baby died, since none of her own kin lived close. "Mama told me once that family reminds you that you have a place in this world," I murmured. "But now that I've seen the world . . . I think I understand what she knew. Friends *can* be like family."

"What about that other girl you've brought in here? Sary?"

I sighed. "Sary and I share a tent at the camp. And her brother, Ben . . . he used to be my friend."

"What happened?"

I hesitated, then the words tumbled out. "The war. It caused all kinds of ugliness. After my mama got beat by the bush-whackers, I thought I had to stop seeing him . . . Ben. I told him so and never gave him a chance to tell his side of things. Then he—he threw stones at us, the day we left."

Mr. Norton shook his head. "I've heard things are bad in the hill country."

"Everybody was going in different directions, and getting angry. Ben's father joined the Confederate Army, and mine joined the Union—oh!" I clapped a hand over my mouth. "I'm sorry. I mean, your foot and all . . ."

He shook his head. "Don't mind. I figured as much. One man in three from East Tennessee went for the Union."

"Do you hate them?" I whispered. "Sometimes I hate my father. For going off and leaving us."

"I once did," he said slowly. "When I woke up in a field hospital in Virginia without my foot . . . yes, I hated all the Yankees. I came back here and then the Yankees occupied Nashville and I hated them all the more."

Sleet hammered at the windows like it wanted to get inside. I poured some more tea. It was a comfort.

Mr. Norton sighed. "I don't hate them anymore. I guess I've forgiven them. They were doing what they felt they had to do." He looked at me. "I hope you can forgive your father one day, Hannah. I expect he was doing what he felt he had to do too."

I brewed that thought. I wanted to forgive him. I truly did! It was the understanding part boxing me in like a thorny fence of Osage orange.

"Forgiving doesn't mean forgetting." Mr. Norton's voice was quiet. "It doesn't mean you weren't hurt, or pretending that you were never angry."

I stared at my fingers.

Mr. Norton opened the stove door, checked the fire, shut it again. "This war has gone on and on. I don't remember what it's all about anymore. I see people going hungry. Children with no place to sleep. I've met many Yankees since they occupied Nashville. Some are small and mean. Others are kind and generous. Some are somewhere in the middle. They're just folks. Same as the Confederates."

"That's the truth." Then I thought of something, and dared a little smile. "And Miss Lynne is a Yankee."

"Yes, she is," he said quietly. "I've learned a lot from Miss

Lynne. She looks at me and somehow sees more than just a Confederate cripple."

"Mr. Norton, are you going to marry Miss Lynne?" The question popped out.

Mr. Norton glared. "And who are you to be asking me such? This is what comes of showing kindness to a ragged girl. Stoke up the fire. And unpack that crate of crackers."

He growled at me for the rest of the morning.

The rain had eased up by midafternoon, but the store was so quiet that Mr. Norton decided to close up shop early. I decided to walk past the Soldiers' Home before going to collect the girls. I hadn't been there since the day I met Dr. Stratton and we quit our jobs with Mr. Reubens. With a bit of luck, the aid ladies would be singing inside.

Lamplight glowed in the Home's windows, and I could hear the piano thumping a goodly distance away. Voices slid out too— a whole group singing something loud with a lot of "glory glory hallelujahs" in it. Shadows were starting to stretch long. I found a good dark spot near the back alley, leaned against the wall, and let the music flow around me like an extra layer to keep me warm. Without the girls to fret about, I could stand here as long as I wanted.

After that piece the ladies sang something that was harder to hear, and then a man sang a sad song about a woman named Lorena. He had a fine voice, and I was enjoying it mightily when the screech and creak and rumble of a handcart sliced through the afternoon. The man dragging the cart down the alley wore a long coat, and a sagging hat pulled down low on his head. "Get some axle grease, mister!" I wanted to say . . . but I knew what it was to work to the bone, in harsh weather. He didn't know he had spoiled my concert.

He stopped the cart by the back entry, tugged up the collar of his coat, and then knocked on the door. After a moment the door swung open, just a bit. "This the Soldiers' Home?" the cartman asked. "I've got some goods, sent down from up north. They told me at the station to bring 'em here."

Something inside of me started to quiver. I pressed tighter against the wall.

Whoever answered the door said something I couldn't hear. "Best let me carry 'em in," the man said. "You know those aid ladies. They cram a crate fuller than full. They're a mite heavy."

My heart skittered fast in my chest. Should I do something? But what? My brain seemed as frozen as my legs, so I didn't move while the man wrestled a crate to the ground, grunting with effort. He heaved it up the step and on into the building.

After the door closed I stood. Someone still pounded the piano, and the men inside were going on about rallying 'round a flag, but I'd lost all joy in the music. It seemed like a long time passed. The sky faded from steel gray toward iron. Finally the door opened again. The cartman came out, waved a hand behind, and whistled as he walked to his rig.

"Willie?" I hadn't known I was going to speak till I heard his name fly out of my mouth.

He went still. Paused a long moment. Finally turned his head. "Who's that?"

I stepped from the shadows. "It—it's me, Hannah." He didn't move. "From last summer."

"Sure, sure, Hannah." His voice was false-cheery. "Say, I've got to get back to the station. Will you walk with me a spell?" He picked up the cart handles and began walking on down the alley. I fell into step beside him. The screech of his wheel like to split my head open.

A block or so away, out on a main street, he pulled the cart tight to the curb and stopped. Only then did he look at me. "Hannah. It's good to see you."

That sounded so silly I almost laughed. Instead I said, voice real low, "Willie, what are you doing in Nashville?"

He blew out a long breath. "You must surely know better than to ask me that."

His business was still secret, then. So why had he gone to the Soldiers' Home? He surely wasn't running guns. He'd delivered something . . . to the Yankees. I pulled Mama's cloak tighter around my shoulders. Or . . . could he have gone inside hoping to *take* something? I thought of Dr. Stratton, making his rounds; the aid ladies writing letters to their friends back home, asking for what they needed. I knew from tales Mr. Norton told that the Confederates were desperate for medicines and hospital supplies. "I was lucky," Mr. Norton had said. "I lost my foot early in the war, when the surgeons still had chloroform."

The lamplighter was making his rounds, and soft pools of light dotted the street. I looked hard at Willie, in his big heavy coat. Had he tucked some supplies in its folds?

"Don't think on it," Willie said evenly. "Just let it go."

And just that quick, I knew he was right. I nodded once and looked him straight on. "Yes. I will."

The tightness in his mouth, his shoulders, eased out. He gave me a true smile. "God's knees, Hannah, you sure surprised me! How are you faring? Where are the young ones?"

"We're getting by. Jasper's working for the railroad. A Northern lady sometimes keeps an eye on the twins. I'll be heading to fetch them soon."

"Good. Good, I'm glad to know you're all right. I've wondered, more than once." He laid a hand on my arm. "Listen, Hannah. I'm truly glad to see you. I owe you an apology."

"You . . . what?"

"Back when you were riding with me, I lost my temper more than once. And I held a grudge. I'm sorry for it."

A couple of Yankees went by, stumbling like they'd somehow found liquor. I felt like I'd snuck into the corn whiskey too. "Willie, I know I hurt your feelings, not telling you about Pa and all. I didn't mean to. I just—I just was trying so hard to keep the kids safe. But—but I'm sorry too."

He grinned so wide I could see it clear in the gloom. "Well, it's just a peach that we ran into each other. I'm glad we could clear the air."

Just like that? So simple? I smiled back. "Willie, don't you have bigger problems to worry about? You saved our lives, you know. I truly do think so. You've got nothing to feel bad about."

Willie shrugged and leaned back against the cart. "We're friends, is all."

Friends. I had two friends now.

Willie crossed one boot over the other, looked away, looked back at me. "I've lost some folks this war, one way or another," he said. "A couple of times I've wished . . . wished I had one more chance to get things right by someone, before they were gone. It can happen so quick." His mouth hardened again. "God Almighty, I hate this war."

I thought of Pa. I had no more chances with him. I thought of Ben.

"Well." Willie straightened up again. "It's fine seeing you, Hannah. It truly is." He stepped between the cart shafts.

"Willie?" I whispered. "Do you hate the Yankees?"

He pondered a long moment before answering. "I hate the ones I don't know. Every one I meet just seems like regular folks."

That's just what Mr. Norton said, I thought. But Willie was doing more than minding a store. "Do you ever wonder if what you're doing is right? I mean—when you've got mean choices to make?"

"No," he said simply. "I can't. It's gotten too hard. I just have to do the best I can. The choices I make . . . someone will likely suffer, either way. I'm on a road, and I've got to walk it."

I watched several mounted Yankees ride by. When the dull clopping of the horse hooves had passed, I said, "I've lied since coming to Nashville. And once I stole food. But I don't know what else I could have done. I purely don't."

"Oh, Hannah," Willie said softly. "There's no right or wrong anymore, that I can see. Your road is rocky too. Make amends where you can, but don't take the war on your shoul-

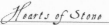

ders." He picked up the long cart handles. "I got to go. Take care, Hannah. Watch out for the little ones."

I stood on the walkway watching him go. I could hear that squeaky wheel long after shadows swallowed Willie. It almost sounded like music.

Meeting Willie made me late picking up the girls that evening. When Mrs. Stratton opened the door, though, she didn't look like she'd minded. "Come in and warm up for a bit. The twins are in the other room. Girls? Get your things on! Hannah's here!"

"Thank you, ma'am." I edged into the warm, cluttered room. A lady I hadn't met before was sitting near the stove, knitting, and she smiled but didn't stop. The aid ladies *would* soon be almost as crowded as we had been at the refugee asylum.

Then Maude came running, and my smile faded. "What's that?"

"A new doll! We each got one." Maude cradled a doll in her arms, pointed toward another sitting on a chair nearby. "Hannah, look! She has a china head, and china hands and feet. Her dress is satin, and she even has a petticoat—"

"Where's Dolly?" I demanded, then turned on Mrs. Stratton. "They already have a doll! Where is their doll?"

"Why . . . it's here somewhere." Mrs. Stratton began looking around, nervously picking up cushions, checking behind chairs. "But Hannah, it's just a doll—I didn't think . . . oh dear, where did it get to. . . ."

The other woman put down her knitting. "Such a fuss! What an ungrateful girl."

I was the one who found Dolly, lying facedown in a corner. I picked her up and saw Mama, bone tired but sitting up by the light of a tallow candle, stitching a gift with work-rough fingers.

"*Here* is your doll." I thrust Dolly at Mary. "This"—I snatched the beautiful new doll Maude was holding away—"does not belong to you."

I don't know that I *meant* to throw it on the floor, but it ended up there. The beautiful china head broke in two, right across the face. "Hannah!" Maude wailed. I looked at the other doll, still sitting on a chair with a calm china smile, and considered throwing that one on the floor too. Mrs. Stratton began weeping. The other woman took a step toward me. I grabbed two thin wrists and half-dragged the girls out the door, down the stairs.

Folks on the street took one look at my thundercloud face and hurried by. We were heading out of the city before I stopped, took a deep breath, and crouched down to face my little sisters. "Girls, I'm sorry. Please stop crying." I heard Willie's voice and was glad he'd gone on, glad he hadn't heard me screech like an angry sow.

Mary patted my hand gently, then Maude's. Her look made my heart ache.

"But why did you break the doll?" Maude wept.

"I—I guess it made me sad to think you didn't want Dolly anymore. Mama made Dolly for you. Don't you remember?"

Maude nodded, but suddenly it struck me that perhaps the twins *didn't* remember, didn't remember Mama at all, didn't remember anything before our miserable life in Nashville. Didn't remember life when the family was all together and the

McNeills felt like true kin, and our only enemies were black bears after our piglets.

I stared blindly at some soldiers trudging by. Finally I became aware of Mary's little hand, still patting mine. "Let's get back," I said heavily, pulling the cape more tightly around her shoulders. "We'll feel better when we've had some supper."

That night I couldn't sleep. "Mama, I gave up the hearth. And I don't think I can hold the family together much longer," I whispered, rubbing the ring. I wished I could wear it. One day, I promised myself, I'll be back on Cumberland Mountain. I will have so much to eat that my fingers will grow, and the ring will fit. Times will be so safe I can wear it. And once that day comes, I will put my mama's ring on my finger and never take it off.

relief crate from the Tennessee Union Orphans and Refugee Relief Society of Bangor, Maine, arrived at our camp at dawn next morning. When the provost marshal doled out the contents, our mess got a sack full of dried apples, another of brown sugar, and a ham. I was too tired to jump into the argument that commenced about that sudden bounty. After the usual bickering the ladies decided to soak the apples, then fry them up with the sugar.

"We'll get a treat this morning," I said to the twins as we ate our regular course of cornmeal mush, hoping it would somehow make up to them for what had happened at the Strattons'.

Then someone called my name—Dr. Stratton himself, walking toward our fire. I felt a push of panic and guilt, all mixed together.

"Good morning," he said when we got up to meet him. He smiled at all three of us, then looked at me. "Hannah, may I speak with you for a few moments?"

I rubbed my arms, considering. "I guess we can sit in our

tent. It's out of the wind. Girls, stay with Sary by the fire. I'll be there in a few minutes."

We still had the two cots pushed together against one canvas wall, so a body had to walk hunched over on the other side where the roof sloped down. I was careful not to touch the tent, but Dr. Stratton bumped his head, and all the icy droplets that had collected on the canvas rained down. I began to fold our ragged quilts and blankets, thrown carelessly aside as we had scampered toward the fire.

He sat on the edge of the cot and took a moment to find words. "Hannah. I'm sorry about what happened yesterday with the dolls."

My hands slowed. "Well . . . I'm real sorry too," I muttered. "I'll pay for the broken one." The words almost choked me.

He waved that aside. "No, no, of course not. But can you tell me why they made you so angry?"

I picked at a tear in one of the quilts. "There's a difference. Between the dolls and everything else you've done for Mary and Maude. You've been wonderful to them," I made myself say. "And I'm beholden. But everything else—all the meals, the shoes, the capes, the new dresses—those were things they needed. They didn't need new dolls. There's a difference."

"I see."

Did he really? I couldn't tell. "It's not that I'm not grateful."

"We made a mistake in buying the dolls." He nodded slowly. "I can see why you felt the way you did."

I felt the weight of a millstone slide from my shoulders. "Good. I'm glad."

I thought that was the end of our talk, but he didn't move. He was still for so long, staring at the ground, that I began to feel nervy inside again. Finally he looked up again. "That's not all I wanted to discuss this morning. You see, my wife is making arrangements to travel back to Iowa. Her health is delicate, and the strain of the living conditions . . . worry about Confederate hopes of retaking Nashville . . . I've decided it's best for her to be at home."

"I hope she gets better, sir."

"Yes, well, I expect she will. But Hannah . . . Mrs. Stratton would like—that is, we both would like it very much if the twins went to Iowa with her."

All the ice in Tennessee got sucked to the pit of my stomach. "You mean . . . to visit?"

He took my hand in his. "No, Hannah. To live. We're offering to adopt Maude and Mary."

I snatched my hand away.

Dr. Stratton began talking very fast. "I understand how you feel. I commend you for it. But I'm asking you to think of the girls. Think what we can offer them. They will always have a safe, warm place to live, away from the war and the fighting. Three good meals a day. All the clothes they need. They can go to school—"

"No!"

"Hannah, you're the adult. I know you love the twins. But you have to think of their best interests—"

"I can take care of the twins!"

"I've seen how you take care of them," he said quietly. "I

know you've done your best. But do you want Mary and Maude to be cold and hungry? Grubbing in the streets for trash? It's not your fault you were born into poverty, Hannah. But we're offering them a future."

"I can give them a future!" I wanted to shout. But the words didn't come, because I knew in my heart I had no future to promise. For a moment we sat still, the only sounds coming from the women and kids clattering around the fire outside. Finally I asked, "What about family? I'm their sister, and Jasper is their brother. That counts for something."

"Yes, of course." He studied his fingers. "Hannah, I'm sorry I can't offer you better. I wish we could take all four of you. I truly do. But we can't. I do well enough on my army salary, but there are difficulties. . . . Of course you'd stay in touch, though. Write letters—that is, do you know how to read and write? Perhaps someone—"

"I know how to read and write," I snapped. "But I want more of my sisters than *letters*." The word tasted sour as vinegar.

"I know this isn't easy. But nothing about your life has been easy. You're a strong girl, Hannah Cameron. I believe you're strong enough to do what's right for Maudie and Mary. I believe you love them enough to want the best for them. To let them go."

Mary poked her head in the tent. Her cheeks were bright red, and she held two tin cups in her hands. "Hannah, they sliced up the ham, and the apples are done! I brought you your share!"

I could no more have eaten that treat than eaten a stone. "You girls have mine," I managed. "Run on back by the fire."

"Thank you, Hannah!" she said happily, and trotted away.

I wanted to hang my head. Everything he said was true. The best I could offer my sisters was a bit of ham and dried apples in sugar, eaten out in the cold, and even that only due to the charity of strangers.

I couldn't look at him. I was out of words. I sat hunched on the edge of the cot, as far away from him as could be.

"Well, you take some time and think about what I've said." Dr. Stratton pushed to his feet, edged toward the front, pushed open the flap. "My wife isn't leaving for almost two weeks. We have plenty of time to make the arrangements. We'll talk again." Then he was gone.

Soon as I was able, I wiped my face and slipped from the tent. I went first to the spring where we washed dishes, and splashed burning-cold water on my face. Then I rejoined the group at the fire.

"Sary, will you watch Maude and Mary today?" I asked, and Sary nodded.

The twins exchanged worried glances. "But where are you going?" Mary asked.

"Into the city," I said, then walked away before they could ask any more questions I didn't have the answers to. I needed to walk, and to think. And for once, I couldn't do that with them. I needed to think this all through without their hands in mine.

I walked and walked and walked. The sun came out, and it warmed up, and I hardly noticed. I walked by the wharves, remembering our first terrible night in Nashville. I walked all the busy streets and narrow alleys where we'd searched for cigar ends. I walked past the Lebanon Turnpike, where Willie had let us off outside of the city, and the Soldiers' Home.

With every step, Dr. Stratton's words pounded in my head, in my heart. *I believe you love them enough to want the best for them. To let them go.* But the notion was still unbearable, and so I kept walking. My head hurt. My heart hurt. I'd thought I could never feel worse than the day we laid my mama in her lonely grave, but I'd been wrong. Over and over wrong. I'd had no choice in Mama dying. Now *I* had to decide whether to give Maude and Mary away.

Finally I trudged up the steep hill toward the state capitol building. The capitol yard was muddy, full of ruts. Barricades blocked civilians from the actual building, but as long as I didn't get too close to the soldiers and such, no one minded a lone girl. I knew where a quiet spot was, beside an old oak tree. It faced east.

I was almost to the tree before I noticed that someone was already there, sitting on the ground, leaning against the trunk. "Oh!" I said, and he turned his head.

"Hannah?" Ben scrambled to his feet. "How did you know to find me here?"

"I wasn't looking for you! I just—just came here. To sit for a while." My voice came out bedraggled as a cat in the rain.

"Well . . . I guess you can sit too," Ben allowed, and sat back down. After a moment I did too, padding the cloak to keep me off the damp ground.

"Why aren't you at work?" I asked after a moment.

"I skipped out." He shrugged, avoiding my gaze. "I've done

that once or twice since coming to Nashville. 'Most always I'm
either working or taking care of Sary. Every once in a while I just
like to come up here and look—"

"Look toward home."

"Yes, look toward home." He pointed. "I know it's too far to
see. But I can imagine it."

"Me too." Below us Nashville spread between our hill and
the Cumberland River, unwinding into the distance. Beyond the
city, beyond the buzzing sawmills and clattering train yards and
pitiful refugee camps, were fields and farms and villages . . . and
in the distance, the dark fins of the foothills, leading toward our
home.

Ben picked up an acorn and threw it down the hill. "Why
did you come to Nashville, Hannah?"

I closed my eyes for a moment. "Well, Mama died . . . and
the neighbors were going to split us up. So we decided—well, I
guess I did most of the deciding—to come here. We were supposed to find Aunt Ellen. Only Aunt Ellen had died."

He nodded. "We got word that my pa had been killed, just
before we got burned out. My mama had a cousin here. That's
why she wanted to come. But Sary and I never could find the
cousin. I don't know whether she died or just up and moved.
Our mule had died, two days out of Nashville, so here we were."

"I wish we'd never left Cumberland Mountain."

"Me too."

We'd each been talking to the sky. For the first time we dared
a quick, sideways look at each other. After all the mess with the
Strattons, I'd almost forgotten my surprise visit with Willie

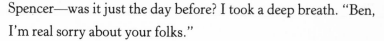

Spencer—was it just the day before? I took a deep breath. "Ben, I'm real sorry about your folks."

"I'm sorry about yours."

"And . . . I'm sorry your place got burned down. Real sorry. Was it the Yankees? Or bushwhackers?"

He shrugged. "I don't even know. Doesn't much matter. End was the same." Then he took a deep breath. "What happened to your mama?"

"Heart got her. Bushwhackers shot in the window one night. The night the Yankees came." I took a deep breath. "Didn't you know?"

"No!" he cried. "No, of course not. Did you think I did? Did you think—"

"Well, I didn't know for sure. The bushwhackers came round more than once. You were all on the same side."

"You were on the same side as the ones who burned us out," he shot back. "And you were the one who got so hateful, that day we were supposed to go hunting."

I hung my head. I remembered it so well. *We Camerons know the difference between right and wrong. . . .* "I wasn't half so smart as I thought I was," I admitted. "But you didn't have to throw rocks at us that day! Why did you?"

"I don't know," he said simply. "I've wished a million times I could just take that whole morning back."

And if I was deep-down honest, I knew I'd had moments along our road to Nashville when I would have rounded on Ben with stones too, if he'd happened by. "I . . . I wish it hadn't all turned out this way," I mumbled to my lap. "You and me feeling like strangers. So many times . . . I just wanted like anything to talk to you."

"Me too." He studied the ground. "I guess I could've tried harder. I guess . . . I was ashamed. You know. About the stones."

I swallowed hard, and looked him in the eye. "Ben, truth is, it—it all started with me. I'm sorry I broke my promise to be friends always. And said such mean things."

"I'm sorry too. About everything."

For a moment we just sat, trying the air now that all those sorrys were out. I sucked in a deep, sweet breath and sent a silent thank-you to Willie Spencer, wherever he was.

Then I remembered Dr. Stratton, and the sweetness was gone. "You know what? I don't even care about all that anymore. It's done. Behind. I've got bigger problems right now."

A shout of laughter drifted across the yard from the soldiers' tents. Ben tossed another acorn down the slope. I watched a red-tailed hawk soaring and diving over the Cumberland and wished I could fly too. "What problems?" he asked.

I wiped my nose on a sleeve. "Dr. Stratton and his wife want to take Maude and Mary to Iowa. I don't even know where that is, but it must be far. They don't want me, or Jasper. And Jasper is so happy working with the railroad men, I think he'll stay on doing that. I knew a woman at the refugee asylum—Mrs. O'Donnell—she lost her son that way."

"I know Jasper does good at his job," Ben admitted. "He's been there longer than me, so he knows the men better. They like him, I can tell. And he likes them. And the engines."

"Yes." I pictured Jasper growing older, staying with the railroad, one day driving a huge smoking locomotive and seeing amazing sights beyond all my imaginings. Like China, and Iowa. "It scares me to have him riding the trains, with the war and all. I know you and Jasper thought we were being silly, that day—"

Ben shook his head. "I did at first. Then I saw how scared Sary was." He smacked one fist into his palm. "I hate leaving her alone so much while I work. We've had some close escapes. Like at the refugee asylum, when they shipped everyone out so fast. She needs to be with me." He looked at me. "Are you going to let Dr. Stratton take the girls?"

"He said that if I loved them, I'd want the best for them."

"Do you think going to Iowa is best for them?"

"I don't know!" I rubbed my forehead. "I know that . . . I know that being alone is the worst feeling. Maybe that's what I'm most scared of." I spread my hands, palms up. "But Mama did want us together. The day she died, she asked me to guard our place and keep the family together. I've made a hash of it, though. Maybe I should mind Dr. Stratton. Do what he wants." The words tasted like unripe persimmons.

"What do *you* want?"

"All I want is to go back home. Try to get the farm going. But we don't have nearly enough money to get back." I blew on my fingers, then stuck them in my armpits. "Besides, we barely made it when Mama was alive. Jasper's a hard worker, but he can't do all the fieldwork himself. And I can't cook and wash and watch the twins *and* help with the crop work too."

Ben pulled a brown leaf to bits. "All I've thought about since we got here was getting Sary back home and trying to pick up again. She's a hard worker too. But she can't do all the cooking alone, and I can't do all the fieldwork by myself *and* help her inside. It's too much."

I don't know who got the idea first. We looked at each other. Looked away. I opened my mouth, shut it again. The words were too fragile. Once spoken, they could never be taken back.

"I need to get on to work," Ben said finally. I watched him push a stray curl behind his ear. Maybe. Just maybe.

"I'm going to walk for a while," I said. "I'm getting too cold to sit."

We scrambled down the hill in silence. When we got to the corner where he turned off, Ben paused. "It was good talking to you, Hannah." I nodded, holding his gaze.

I didn't get back to the refugee camp, footsore and frozen, until suppertime. Only two women were huddled by the fire in our row of tents. They stopped talking when they saw me and deep-dark stared. My stomach knotted.

One came to meet me. "Hannah," she began. "Oh, child." Her mouth worked, but nothing else came out. This was a woman quite capable of talking the horns off a cow.

I began to run.

They thought it was the ham. Not cured right, maybe. Or maybe it just sat too long on some railway platform on that long journey from Maine to Tennessee. All I knew was that I hadn't eaten any that morning. *You girls have my share,* I'd said. . . .

That evening I kept trying to wake up from a bad dream. I remember slipping beneath the tent flap. Sary and another woman knelt by one of the cots. The twins lay together, bundled beneath quilts. Maude had one arm over Mary. "Hannah," Maude whimpered, looking up at me. But Mary didn't call my name or even open her eyes. I could tell from the sour bedding just how sick she was. Every breath sounded heavy. When I touched her forehead, it felt like July.

I remember the kind tone one of the women used to tell me about that long day. "Everybody who ate that ham took sick, soon after breakfast. Some a lot worse than others. Your girls puked it all up, same as the rest. Maude, she's just fine now. But this little one got took bad. . . ."

I remember the camp doctor coming, sometime after the sun had set. He hung a lantern from the ridgepole before looking at the girls. "This one's no better than she was this afternoon." He sighed. "Was she already sick?"

"Not to speak of. Not lately." My lips felt like ice. The insides of my bones felt like ice. The doctor said something about "prolonged weakened condition" and laid a heavy hand on my shoulder.

I remember Maude whispering, sometime later, "Hannah, is Mary going to die?"

"No!" I blazed. *No.*

A flutter of movement caught my eye. Mary's hand found Maude's. I picked up Mary's other hand. I could feel every bone through her skin.

"As I walked out one evening fair," I began to sing, "out of sight of land, there I saw a mermaid a-sitting on a rock, with a comb and a glass in her hand." My voice was as soft as the fingers I used to smooth Mary's hair, as I had a hundred-hundred nights before. I sang every song I knew. A couple of the women came and went, coaxing some water between Mary's lips, giving Maude a bite of soft bread. Someone tried to give me some too, but I shoved it away.

And I remember that I was in the middle of "The Camerons Are Coming" when one of those women pulled Mary's little hand from mine and laid it on the quilt. "Hannah," she murmured, "you got to let go."

I shoved her away, real fierce. "You don't understand, she gets sickly from time to time, but she always gets better—"

"Hannah," the woman said, firm this time. "Hannah, come away. Mary's gone."

I sat still as stone on Sary's cot with Maude in my lap, watching those good women ready Mary for burial in the morning. The lantern light cast long shadows on the tent canvas. Every breath I drew hurt somewhere deep in my chest. I wished I could just stop breathing altogether.

Finally I became aware of Maude's trembling. It was more than chill-shivers. Little shudders rippled through her body. I hugged her tight and pulled another quilt around her shoulders, but she didn't stop.

"Maudie," I whispered. "Maude?"

Maude didn't look at me. Didn't speak.

And I reached the bottom of my well. I grabbed Maude

up, still wrapped in her shawl and cape and a quilt, and headed outside.

No one stopped me. I wasn't used to roaming in the dark of night, but I knew where I was going. When we entered Nashville proper the hissing streetlamps helped me along. I had to stop and rest more than once, but soon enough I was climbing the stairs of the brick house on College Street. When I got to the top I let Maudie slide gently to the ground. Her nose was running, but she never sniffled. She had a look in her eyes like a doe I saw once, rifle-shot but not down.

I banged on the door. "Mrs. Stratton!" I hollered. "Mrs. Stratton!"

After a moment I heard voices beyond the door. It opened a crack. I saw a lamp's glow, saw Miss Lynne peeking out. "I need to see Mrs. Stratton," I said.

The door opened wider, and the doctor's wife pushed forward. She wore a dark wrapper over her nightdress, and a thick braid hung over one shoulder. "Hannah? What on earth—"

"Take her," I cried, scooping up Maude and all her layers.

"But—"

"*Take her!*" I gave Maude a fierce hug, and kissed the top of her head, before easing her into Mrs. Stratton's arms.

The pain in my chest threatened to swallow me whole. I didn't want to crumble there. Not there. I turned my back and fled.

When I got back to the refugee camp Jasper and Ben were waiting. I grabbed Jasper and squeezed him close. I felt his muscled-up shoulders through his coat and smelled the smoke in his hair.

Finally he pulled away. Over his shoulder I saw Ben, his eyes dark and sad.

"How did you know?" I whispered.

"Sary came and got us."

I nodded my gratitude at Sary, then looked back to Ben.

He bit his lip. "Oh, Hannah." Somehow I ended up with my face crushed into his shoulder. He smelled of smoke too, and sweat. When I felt his hard arm circle my shoulders, the tears finally broke free. I cried and cried and cried. "I know," he said, stroking my hair.

"I want to go home!" I sobbed.

"I know."

"I—can't—do—this—anymore!"

"I know."

"I want to go *home!*"

He stroked my hair again. "We will."

CHAPTER 19

We buried Mary in the morning, in the little cemetery that had sprung up at the edge of the camp. The army provided a coffin. One of the soldiers even read a piece from the Bible. And all those refugee ladies were kind as could be.

Mr. Norton came out in a hired pony cart to pay his respects. "I am so, so sorry," he said, and gave me a big hug, and let me cling to his hand.

Dr. Stratton came out too. He looked torn up.

"Oh, Hannah," he said heavily.

"How's Maude?" I managed. I ached for the twins like a dry creek bed aches for rain.

"She's . . . she was sleeping when I left. We didn't think it was wise to bring her out again." Dr. Stratton stood over that fresh little grave for a few minutes, with his head bowed. Then he blew his nose and went back to Nashville.

I borrowed a kettle and did laundry, scrubbing the sickness out of Mary's quilt. The rest of the day I spent lying on the cot.

My cot now.

Jasper stayed for a while, grim and silent, then disappeared. Ben let me be until sometime in the afternoon. He poked under the tent flap. "Hannah? Can we talk for a spell?" He sat down on Sary's bed.

"I don't feel much like talking." I curled on my side, staring at one of his muddy boots. The toe stitching was coming loose.

"Well . . . just listen, then." He paused for a long while. Then, "I wasn't just talking, what I said before. I think we might be able to do it."

"Do what?"

"Go home."

The dull ache in my chest made it hard to think straight. I had a fuzzy memory of thinking the same thing. *Daring* to think it. "Together . . ."

"Yes!" he said urgently. "Together. *Together* I think we can do it. Between us, Jasper and I could manage the heavy work."

It was just what I had been thinking—before. "I could cook, and garden. Sary can help. . . ." I buried my head in my arms. "But not without Mary," I wept. "All this time of wishing and working, I never figured it would be without Mary." And without Maude.

"I know." Ben put a hand on my shoulder for a bit. "Just think on it, Hannah. We'll talk again."

That night inched by. Next morning, Jasper and Ben headed back to work.

I spent that whole week lying on my bed. I couldn't remember ever doing *nothing* before. Ever. But aside from crawling to the sinks when I needed to, I didn't have it in me to move.

Each evening when the boys came back, Jasper'd sit with me for a while. Ben always stopped by too. "I can't think on anything yet," I'd tell him, and he'd go on again.

On the seventh evening, when Jasper was eating supper by the fire, Ben came in and flipped one of the canvas flaps open. I scrunched my eyes against the light and huddled deeper under the quilt. Ben sat down. "Hannah. You got to start thinking now. It's time."

"I can't—"

"Yes, you can. It's time."

It wasn't time. It would *never* be time. But Ben didn't leave. After a bit, I sat up.

Ben leaned close, elbows on his knees. "About heading back. I figure we'll just farm one place, to start. Probably yours, since our cabin got burned down."

"Our . . . our smokehouse and pigpen got burned down."

"But between us, we have what we need."

I hitched the quilt closer around my shoulders. Star of Bethlehem, my ma had called this pattern. I swallowed hard. "I—I haven't asked Jasper yet. I don't know that he'll be coming."

Ben frowned, pondering that through. "Well . . . I guess I could handle the farm work alone. Yes. I did it before, after my pa went off."

"Ben . . . that's something else we got to get around. You and Sary are Confederates. I'm a Yankee. We got to talk about that."

"I guess you're right," he said slowly. "Me and Sary *are* Confederate. I would never turn my back on my pa's memory.

But I got to say . . . beyond that, I don't really know what it means."

From beyond the canvas wall I could hear voices from the camp. "She stole my frypan!" someone screeched.

"I've been trying for the longest time to figure out why my pa chose for the Union," I said finally. "I've talked to a bunch of Union soldiers, and still don't know. I'm glad the Union Army freed the slaves, but in truth I don't think that's why Pa left. Anyway, I can't turn my back on his memory either."

"My pa didn't fight to hang on to slavery, you know!"

"I never said he did," I said wearily. Mr. McNeill had been a fierce, independent man like Pa. Neither would have had any use for slaves, or the notion of 'em. But I noticed Ben didn't say why his father *had* joined the Confederate Army. Maybe he didn't know either. Or maybe it truly didn't matter anymore.

"A . . . a friend of mine told me not to take the war on my shoulders," I said. "Ben, I can't pretend the war hasn't changed things. But I know we're both sorry about it. I can live with that."

"I can live with that too." For a moment his eyes shone, and I saw a spark of the old Ben. Then it died again. "What do you suppose has been going on at home?" he asked. "I'm hoping that once we get back the Rebels won't bother us on account of me and Sary, and the Yankees won't bother us on account of you. But truth is, things could go just the other way."

"I know. Are you willing to chance it?"

"Yep."

"Me too." Something eased, deep in my chest—just the tiniest bit. "But first we have to *get* back."

"I know, I know." Ben drummed his fingers on his knees. "But I've been thinking on it. We need a mule, and a cart. And enough money for some supplies."

"It's too much."

"Don't give up yet. I've been saving since we got here. It's not much. But it's a start. How much have you got?"

I heaved myself up, tied the tent flaps closed, and poured the contents of my hidden pocket on the bed. "It's not even close. I've spent enough time in Mr. Norton's store to know that. We'll have to keep saving. Maybe in another year—"

"I can't wait another year," Ben said flatly. He fingered the coins, figuring in his head. "I think between us we have enough here for the supplies we need to get back home, and for some seed corn and potatoes. We need those, since we can't count on finding anything left at your place. And I think I can get us a mule."

"You can?" I stared at him. "They're terribly dear, even if you can find one! The army has taken every horse and mule for miles!"

"You're right. But sometimes they work 'em too hard. They keep a stable yard south of town, where they take worn-out horses and mules. I've been there. Some of them are still sound. I think I can get us one that could get us back to Cumberland Mountain, and pull a plow."

"But how can you pay for it?"

Ben took a deep breath. "I started going there soon after Sary and I got here. I got to know one of the mule drivers. And once I showed him this." He reached inside his coat pocket and pulled out a tiny pistol. It was the prettiest gun I'd ever seen. "This belonged to my great-grandfather. The driver said he'd trade me a mule for it. A good mule."

I stared. "Oh, Ben . . ."

He swallowed hard but waved my protest aside. "So we can get a mule, and supplies. That just leaves the cart. We have to figure out how to get a cart."

"With so many refugees on the roads, carts can't be easy to come by." I lay down again.

"Just think on it," Ben said. He could be mule-stubborn too.

We decided not to tell Sary and Jasper of our plans until we had everything worked out. Then Ben looked me straight in the eye. "Is Maude coming with us?"

I looked at the stained canvas. "I'm not fit to keep her. She'd be better off with the Strattons."

Ben twisted his mouth.

"Ben . . . do you think it's my fault Mary died?"

"It's nobody's fault. Or maybe it's everybody's—the ones who started the war, and the men who shot out your windows that night, even them that sent the ham. The way I see it, all a person can do is make the best choices they know how, every minute."

I curled back down on the quilt. "I used to watch Mama and Aunt Ellen laugh together, and whisper together, and I wanted a sister too. When the twins were born, I figured out quick enough they didn't need me for much. I'm not sure I ever quite forgave them for that." I couldn't look at Ben. "I guess I'm not much good at being on my own."

After a minute Ben said, "You don't have to be."

"What do you think?" I whispered, finally looking back at him. "Tell me what to do! I don't know what's right!"

He opened his mouth, then shut it again. Finally he shook his head. "I'm thinking you do."

I didn't have the energy to puzzle that out. Or maybe I didn't have the courage yet to face what he was telling me. I pressed my cheek into the quilt. "Well, Mrs. Stratton isn't leaving for another week."

"If we're going to do this, we need to know by then anyway. We have to get back in time to get crops in the ground."

Ben went off to find his own supper. I reached into a basket below the bed and pulled out Dolly. I hadn't thought to grab her when I'd hauled Maude off to the Strattons. I touched the worn face, the tattered clothes, seeing Mary and Maude. "Oh, Mama," I whispered. "I'm so sorry. I miss them so much."

Sary brought me a plate, and I ate a few bites before putting it aside and reaching again for that doll. *Dolly.* I remembered the day I'd broken one of the store-bought dolls the Strattons got for the twins. I'd been so angry, remembering how Mama had worked on Dolly. . . .

No, wait. There was more to it than that.

I went to sleep that night with my fingers curled around Mama's wedding ring. *Mama,* I told her, *I'm trying to sort everything out.*

CHAPTER 20

When I opened my eyes, I knew what I was going to do. Maybe Mama had whispered in my ear while I slept. Or maybe it just took me some time to accept the notion that precious things are expensive. Now I knew that, bone deep.

Still, knowing didn't make it easy. My fingers shook as I braided my hair, before going out to the morning campfire for the first time in a week. Sary smiled nervously, patting the log beside her. One of the women made sure I got my share of corn-meal mush and salt pork, but my stomach was so churned up with nerves it was hard to choke it down.

I headed first to the refugee asylum at the Shelby Medical College. A few tents were pitched in the yard. That meant the entire building was crammed with new refugees. I wondered if Mrs. O'Donnell would ever see her son again, and if that slave woman we'd met would ever find any kin. Too many families torn to bits. I was done with it.

I waited in the yard, pacing. The sun had disappeared behind another gray sky, and I stamped my feet, blowing on my fingers, willing him to come quickly. Finally, just when I was afraid I had somehow missed him, Dr. Stratton came out the front door.

"Dr. Stratton!" I hurried across the yard to meet him.

"Why, Hannah! I didn't expect you—let's go back inside—"

"No thank you, sir. This won't take long." I took a deep breath and plunged ahead. "I just came to tell you that the answer is no. About Maude, I mean."

His eyes went wide. "But—but you already gave her to us," he stammered. "We were planning to see you before she left, of course, but—"

"I'm ever so sorry for giving you the wrong idea," I said, clenching my hands in my skirt to keep them from trembling. "I truly needed help the night Mary died. You gave it, and I'm thankful. But you can't keep Maude."

"But . . ." He looked bewildered.

"It was a most kind offer. Please give my thanks to Mrs. Stratton. For everything." I shifted my weight from one foot to the other.

He stared at me. "But—but why?" he asked finally. "We have so much to give!"

"But me and Jasper and Maude, we're family. And you never gave much mind to me and Jasper."

"You and Jasper are older, you can find work. . . ." But his face flushed red as a maple tree in autumn. He cleared his throat. "Shouldn't we discuss this with Maude?"

"No sir," I said firmly. "Maude is a child. I'm the oldest. You said so yourself. I made the decision for her."

"But Hannah—" He shook his head, stumbling for words. "Your choice means a hard life for Maude. A much harder life. Do you really want to make that sacrifice for her?"

"Sometimes people have to make sacrifices to hold the family together."

"I see." He shook his head, and his mouth grew hard. "Hannah, I must say I think you're being selfish. Even cruel. The truth is . . . well, I hate to say this, but if you'd left the twins with us earlier—"

"Dr. Stratton." My skin prickled, and I felt dizzy, so I spread my feet a bit wider apart and faced him down like a long row to plow. "I got to carry what happened, but how I do that is my choice. There's only one thing I know for sure, and that's that all a person can do is make the best choices they can, every minute. I've done that all along, and I'm doing that now."

"You're young. You should—"

"Let me ask you something," I said. "Why do you suppose my mama only made one doll for the twins?"

His face got red again. "Well, I suppose she . . . she was busy, or . . . she couldn't afford cloth for two."

"Mama made one doll because she knew Mary and Maude were two halves of one whole. Mama understood that. Dr. Stratton, you can give Maude lots of things. But I know who she is. All the china dolls in the world won't make up for that."

"I see," he said again. His voice was stiff. But the look in his eyes told me he was more grieving than angry.

"Dr. Stratton . . . there are lots of children like Maude. I hope this doesn't make you too sad to look after someone else. Find someone who doesn't already have an older sister to tend her."

He managed a weak smile. "Yes. Perhaps we will."

"If you could let your wife know, I'll come by this evening for Maude." I left him standing in the yard.

From the asylum I walked the familiar streets to Norton's store. My stomach still felt a bit trembly, but my feet made long strides. I felt ready to look God Himself in the eye if I had to.

I found Mr. Norton behind the counter, wrapping an ounce of headache powder in a twist of paper for an old woman. The clouds were so low outside that he'd lit a lamp on the counter so he could see his ledger, and I waited while he scratched the entry in the book.

"Hannah, I'm so glad to see you," he said when the customer was gone. "I've been thinking about you. How are you?"

"I'm making on." I faced him square across the counter. "Mr. Norton, are you going to ask Miss Lynne to marry you?"

He folded his arms. "I told you before that it's no concern—"

"I don't mean to be disrespectful," I interrupted. "But I know you're going to propose to her, Mr. Norton. I've seen you together. I can tell."

"Well—"

"I know you'll want everything just right. Just perfect. The way she would want it. And you'll need a ring." I took a deep breath. "Not just any ring. A special ring, just for Miss Lynne."

I reached beneath my collar and pulled out the string. When the ring came loose I held it out for Mr. Norton to see. The green stone sparkled in the lamplight.

"Good gracious!" Mr. Norton stared like he'd seen a sign from heaven. "That's an emerald! Wherever did you get that ring?"

"From my mama. It's mine to do with what I please."

"Oh, Hannah . . . you shouldn't even think of giving up that ring! I know you set a store by your family, and if that's all you've got to remember her by—"

"I do set a store by family. I'm trying to put together a new one." I found a smile for my friend. "And I want you to have this ring for Miss Lynne."

Mr. Norton touched the ring, then shook his head. "I'm sorry, Hannah. It is a beautiful ring. And you're right, it's perfect for Miss Lynne. But I can't pay you what it's worth." He gestured toward his almost-empty shelves. "The war—"

"I don't need you to pay me what it's worth. I want to trade you for it."

He brightened. "What do you want? Food?"

"A mule cart."

"A mule cart!"

"Yes. A small one will do. Two-wheeled." I squeezed my hands into fists. I'd gotten through the hardest part. Now I felt like I was standing on the edge of something powerful and wonderful. All I needed was Mr. Norton's help to make it all come true.

"I don't have a cart—"

"But you know lots of people. Farmers, merchants—everyone you do business with. You can find one."

"Times are hard. Vehicles are scarce." But he was staring at the ring.

"I know you can do it, Mr. Norton."

I waited. He stared. Finally he slammed his hand down on the counter. "You've got a deal."

The night before we left Nashville, our last night in the refugee camp, we piled our precious barrel of cornmeal and sacks of seed corn and sweet potatoes in the cart so we could get an early start. Toward morning a storm blew in. I lay in the tent and listened to the rain beat on the canvas overhead, remembering the rainstorm of our first night on the road.

At the first flush of dawn I slipped out of the tent and walked to the graveyard to say good-bye to Mary. "I purely hate having you rest here, so far from home," I told her. "But I know that your spirit's with Mama and Pa. And I'll do the best I can by Maudie. I promise you that."

When I walked back I found Ben peering anxiously under the oilcloth he'd stretched over the top of the cart. "Dry," he announced. "But we need to weight this oilcloth better. Grab some rocks."

We scrabbled in the mud, but for an instant the world spun around and I saw Ben's hands closing around a stone, ready to throw. "Don't!" I cried. Then the world spun back to normal, with Ben staring like I'd gone addled. I rubbed my forehead. "Never mind."

It will take some getting used to, I thought, as we got on with it. Ben and I'd been the closest friends before all the trouble started. It stood to reason that the ugliness cut us the deepest.

When we had the cart tucked up tight I managed a smile.

But Ben pulled off his battered hat, ran a hand over his hair, chewed his bottom lip. "I don't know, Hannah," he muttered. "I was awake 'most all last night. We've got a long way to go, and Lord only knows what we'll find when we get there. What if bushwhackers have burned down your cabin too? What'll we do then?"

I laid a hand on his arm. "Then we'll go fetch that hearthstone you gave me," I told him. "It's tucked away safe. We'll build from that if we need to."

His shoulders lost their bunched-up look. His mouth hinted toward a smile. He held my gaze, and for the first time in ever so long, that was all we needed. Then Sary ran to meet us, with Jasper and Maude coming along behind.

Maude had been wearing a whole new outfit when I picked her up, so clean and spruced I hardly recognized her. But she'd run to me, and I sent up a prayer of thanks for that. She still wasn't talking, though, and she'd scarce been a step away from my skirt. I knew she'd spend the rest of her life figuring out how to get along without Mary.

She looked so lost that I took her hand. *I'll help you find your way*, I tried to tell her with a squeeze. *Everybody will—me and Jasper, and Ben and Sary too. I know it will take a lot of getting used to. But I think we can do it.*

Jasper would have to get used to working a farm with Ben, instead of Pa. He'd been surprised by my plan. Then quiet, a long thinking quiet that rattled my nerves. "I don't know, Hannah," he said finally. "I've been figuring on staying with the railroad. It's good work."

"I know," I said. "And I won't tell you what to do. You've taken good care of us already, just like Pa would have wanted. It's up to you to decide."

"I suppose I could come back to the railroad one day," Jasper said slowly. "Even if I come help get the farm going. The fields will be a mess."

I nodded. "Sure enough, you could. But I'll tell you plain, Jasper, I don't know how it's going to be. You already know how long a walk it is. Our mule could get stolen again, or somebody could get snakebit, or food might run scarce. And we don't know what we'll find when we get back home. Me and Ben are hoping that between us we'll keep off all the bushwhackers, but truth is, we might just make everybody angry. Maybe both sides'll come down on us—"

"Hannah!" Jasper looked dazed. "You trying to talk me into going, or into staying?"

I took a deep breath. "I'm trying to be fair. Coming out, I told rosy tales about how easy everything would work out. And I was wrong every step of the way. You're pulling your weight for this family, Jasper, and I aim to do better by you this time."

He planted his feet and folded his arms, looking for all the world like Pa. "All right. I'll go back with you."

"Thank you." I gave his shoulder one quick squeeze. "After . . . after Mary, I couldn't bear to lose you too. Not just yet."

"Well, I couldn't allow you and Maude to head back without me," he added, warming up to the idea. "It's too far. I'd be afraid I'd never see you again."

"I'm grateful, Jasper. And I won't forget your feelings.

Sometimes people have to make sacrifices to hold the family together."

Those were the same words I said to Dr. Stratton about Maude, I thought, as I remembered that talk with Jasper. _Sometimes people have to make sacrifices to hold the family together._ Where had they come from? Then I remembered Pa, saying those very words to me the morning he left to march off to war, long ago.

_Oh, Pa . . ._ I scarcely breathed, remembering, trying to sort it out. At the time, I thought Mama and Jasper and Mary and Maude and me were the only ones making a sacrifice. I'd hardly listened to what he was trying to say. Oh, what had it been! I closed my eyes, trying to remember. _I'm for the Union_, Pa had said. _It's like a family. A clan. Sometimes people have to make sacrifices to hold the family together._ Pa had known that folks could hold different ideas and still get along, like me and Ben were trying to do. Once a family got broken, there was no telling how many pieces might fall away.

Ben and I—we could do this.

"Hannah Cameron! You planning on standing there asleep all day, or you planning to start heading for home?" Ben was tucking up the last corners of the cart, watching me.

I blinked and looked around. Jasper was harnessing the new mule. The girls were waiting. Some of the other refugee women stood watching, looking happy and worried for us, and some powerful envious too.

"Everyone ready?" I called. "Let's get moving!"

———

We made about ten miles that day—good time, considering we weren't used to traveling. I could feel Mary traveling with us. Somehow she didn't feel so far away as Mama, or Pa. I watched Maude, jouncing along in the cart, and realized that we'd always have something of Mary left, something real. It was a comfort.

It was cold, but spring was in the air. I could smell it, feel it, and I smiled when I pictured the mountains bursting green to meet us. Would we arrive when the redbuds were swelling? When the serviceberry and dogwood were welcoming Preacher to his spring rounds? When the swallows were building their nests under the porch roof? When the frogs at Sandy Spring began their night singing?

We made camp on the banks of a branch of Stones River and had a nice supper of corn cakes and dried apples. We needed to be careful, watch our supplies—but it didn't fret me as much as it had on our trip west. Maybe it was because we were marching toward spring, with the promise of bear lettuce and toothwort and ramps and raspberries waiting to be gathered along the road. Maybe it was because we were heading toward home, instead of away from it. Or maybe, I thought, looking across the fire at Ben, it's because all of the weight isn't on my shoulders.

After supper Jasper took a brush to the mule, making friends. Sary set to with the dishes. I watched, holding my breath, as Maude went to help.

"You want me to snap you off a nice spruce branch to scrub with?" Sary asked. "Gravel works good too." Maude didn't answer. But she pointed at a branch.

Ben looked at me. "Hannah. Let's go skip stones."

"Skip stones! I don't remember how. And the girls—"

"Come on." He pulled me to my feet. "They can see us." We walked to the river's edge. I looked over my shoulder once. Maudie was helping Sary.

"Say," Ben said, "did you notice on the walk west that the salamanders from ridge to ridge were all a little different? Why do you suppose that is? And did you happen to see that huge sycamore near Lebanon that got hit by lightning, and was growing sideways?"

I let his words and wondering pour right down inside until that empty place in my chest filled up and spilled over, all the while searching the bank for a stone. Finally my fingers closed around a good one: flat, about the size of my palm. I hefted it, turned it over. Just right.

"Let's do a double," Ben suggested. "See whose goes the farthest." He chose his stone, and we perched on the bank, ready. The late sun skittered bright on the river. "Go!" Ben shouted. Those stones went dancing across the water, into the sun, out of sight.